The Alden Family Mysteries
by Gertrude Chandler Warner

THE BOXCAR CHILDREN
SURPRISE ISLAND
THE YELLOW HOUSE MYSTERY
MYSTERY RANCH
MIKE'S MYSTERY
BLUE BAY MYSTERY
THE WOODSHED MYSTERY
THE LIGHTHOUSE MYSTERY
MOUNTAIN TOP MYSTERY
SCHOOLHOUSE MYSTERY
CABOOSE MYSTERY
HOUSEBOAT MYSTERY
SNOWBOUND MYSTERY
TREE HOUSE MYSTERY
BICYCLE MYSTERY
MYSTERY IN THE SAND
MYSTERY BEHIND THE WALL
BUS STATION MYSTERY
BENNY UNCOVERS A MYSTERY

Surprise Island

Surprise

Island

by

Gertrude Chandler Warner

Illustrated by

Mary Gehr

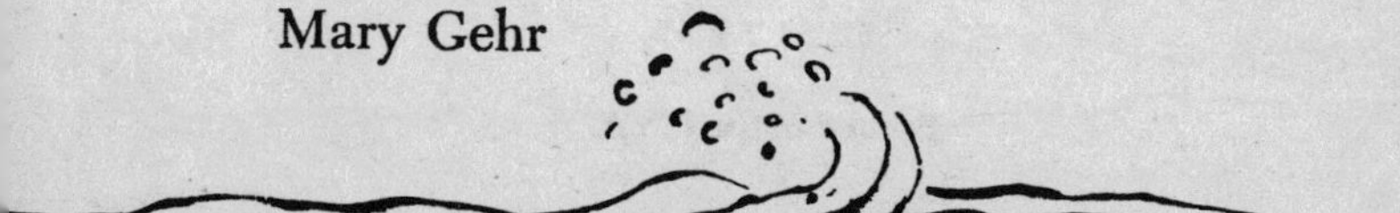

ALBERT WHITMAN & Company, Niles, Illinois

ISBN 0-8075-7674-3

52 54 53 51

Printed in the U.S.A.

Contents

Surprise Island

Chapter 1

The First Surprise

Now, tell us, Grandfather," cried Henry. "We ran all the way home from school."

"Tell us!" shouted Benny, throwing himself down on the grass beside the dog. "School is out for the whole summer, and Watch wants to know."

"Violet and I want to know, too," said Jessie.

Mr. Alden was sitting in the garden reading. He looked at his four grandchildren in surprise.

"Let me see, was this the day I said I'd tell you?" he asked them.

"He's joking, Benny," said Jessie.

"Joking?" cried Mr. Alden. "I mean everything I say!"

But he was joking, just the same, and enjoying himself, too. In the spring, he had promised his grandchildren a surprise for the summer, and now he had been waiting more than an hour for the children to come home.

"School is out," said Violet.

"We ran all the way home," shouted Benny.

"Yes, so you said," said Mr. Alden slowly.

"You said the surprise was something you liked to do yourself when you were fifteen," Henry told him.

"Yes, or even six," said Mr. Alden, looking at Benny.

"And you said you'd tell us the minute school was out, Grandfather," said Benny.

Mr. Alden laughed. "I certainly did," he replied. "And now I'm going to tell you."

The four children looked at him.

He began, "Once upon a time my father bought an island."

"He *bought* one!" cried Henry.

"Yes," Mr. Alden went on. "The island is small.

There is nothing much on it except a small house, a barn, and a fisherman's hut. My father wanted a quiet place to keep his best horses. Old Captain Daniel, who runs the motorboat, lives in the fisherman's hut now. Let's all go down to the island and look it over. If you want to stay there all summer, you may."

"Oh, Grandfather!" cried Jessie. "We would like it better than anything in the world. It will be just like the boxcar days!"

"Couldn't Watch go, too?" asked Benny, with his hand on the dog's head.

"Certainly," said Mr. Alden. "He would be lonesome without you."

"Can we have a real stove, and cook?" asked Violet.

"You'll have to cook," replied Mr. Alden, "if you want to eat. I will give you some money for dishes and things. You must tell me how much money you need, but don't make it too much."

All the children laughed a little, because even

Benny knew that their grandfather had enough money to buy anything they wanted.

"Let's go now," said Benny suddenly.

The four children jumped up so quickly that Mr. Alden threw back his head and laughed.

"We will go in the car as far as the ocean," he said. 'Then Captain Daniel will take us in the motorboat across to the island. We might stop and get Dr. Moore and his mother to come along and enjoy the fun. It's the doctor's day off."

The children were delighted, for Dr. Moore and his mother were their best friends.

Dr. Moore did not look at all surprised when they came. He helped his mother into the big car, and off they all went toward the ocean. On the way Jessie and Violet began to plan their housekeeping.

"We have to buy bread and bottles of milk," said Jessie. "Then we could live, even if we didn't have anything else to eat."

"Here's a little book and a pen," said Mr. Alden, taking a small blue book from his pocket.

"Write down the dishes we need," said Violet.

Before they reached the ocean, Jessie had put down all the things they could think of. There were spoons, cups, bowls, plates, a sharp knife, a dishpan, and a big kettle.

Then they saw the ocean and the Alden motorboat tied up at the small dock. Captain Daniel, the old fisherman, was waiting for them on the dock.

"How are you, Captain?" said Mr. Alden, as they shook hands. "Just take us across to the island. If the children don't like it, you can bring us right back again."

The children shouted at this. "We'll like it all right," they said.

They climbed into the boat and were off.

"There's our island!" cried Henry. "Our very own island!"

Benny began to wave.

"There's nobody there, Benny. Why are you

waving?" asked Grandfather. In spite of this, all the children began to wave at the island.

"And there's our little house!" shouted Benny. "But is it big enough for all of us?"

"Oh, no," said Captain Daniel. "That little hut is my house." He laughed and looked at Mr. Alden.

They landed at the little dock, and walked a short way before they saw a small yellow house.

"Are we going to live in that yellow house?" cried Jessie.

"Oh, no!" answered Mr. Alden. "You children are going to live in the barn!"

"In the barn!" shouted the children, as they ran over to it.

"This is the best idea I have ever heard!" cried Henry. He opened the big door and looked in. A new floor had been laid but the children did not notice it. All of them were looking at the four box stalls along the back of the room.

"Bedrooms!" cried Benny, pointing to the box stalls.

"That's what they are!" said Henry, opening one of the swinging doors to look in. Each stall had a large window and nothing else at all.

"Let's bring down some straw for beds," said Henry, looking up the stairs. "We can cover the straw with blankets." He pointed to a pile of clean, light brown blankets.

Jessie ran over to look at the little stove. It was new, and there was an oven on top. Then Henry walked over to look at some barrels.

"Here are two empty barrels," he shouted. "We can use them for table legs, and lay this long board across them for a table."

"Wonderful!" said Jessie.

The older people stood in the doorway, watching the excited children.

"I'm glad the workmen left these old boxes here," said Henry. "I can make dozens of things out of that wood—maybe a little cupboard for the dishes."

"Oh, Henry, do you think you could?" cried Violet. "We wouldn't need doors."

"Of course he could," said Benny. "He could make doors, too. Henry can make anything."

"There is a little spring over there," said Mr. Alden, taking the children to the window to look. "That spring never runs dry. It is always as cold as ice, even on very hot days, and it is safe to drink, too."

"Isn't this perfect, Henry?" said Jessie. "The most important things are settled already. Oh, I wish we could stay here tonight!"

"How about dishes?" asked Violet.

Jessie said, "We can get spoons and things at the five and ten. Are there any dishes already on the island, Grandfather?"

"Not a dish except what the captain has," replied Mr. Alden. "I'm sorry."

"Don't be sorry!" cried Jessie. "It's lots more fun to buy them. Let's get six of each thing. Then we can have company."

"There's still time to go back to the mainland," said Henry looking at his watch. "We could go to the five and ten for dishes, and we could buy bread and milk for supper."

"And I want my bear," said Benny.

"Very well, my children," said Mr. Alden, smiling. "You shall go back and get your things and stay here this very night."

But just then Mr. Alden noticed that Captain Daniel had something on his mind.

"Did you want something, Captain?" he asked.

"Well, yes," replied Captain Daniel. "I heard you say I was the only one on the island."

"Well, aren't you?" Mr. Alden looked at him.

"No, I'm not. I've got a young friend staying with me in my hut. I thought I had better tell you. He's a good young man, handy and all, but he hasn't been well."

"What's the matter with him? Who is he?" asked Mr. Alden sharply, just as Captain Daniel knew he would.

"I've known him all his life," said Captain Daniel Then he looked at Dr. Moore for help.

"Suppose I go down to the hut and talk with this man," said Dr. Moore.

"Fine!" said Mr. Alden. "You go and see what this is all about."

"I want to go with you," said Benny.

"Oh, no," said the doctor. "You go look in the windows of the yellow house, and see what you can see. I'll be right back."

So the children went over to look into every window, while Dr. Moore went off with Captain Daniel to see his friend.

Chapter 2

Housekeeping

Thank you for coming, Doctor," said Captain Daniel, as they walked toward the fisherman's hut. "You will see that it's all right."

Soon they came to the hut. A young man sat in the door, fixing a lobster pot.

"Hello," he said, looking up.

"Hello," replied Dr. Moore. "I'm a doctor, and I thought I would come to see you. Mr. Alden is leaving his four grandchildren on the island with Captain Daniel."

The young man smiled. "Yes, I know," he said. "I'm glad you came."

"He's a very handy man, Joe is," put in Captain Daniel. "He's a big help to me."

"I'd like to tell you about myself," said the young man. "Please sit down a minute.

"I used to live around here," he went on. "Last year I went off to explore a place, and dig up old Indian things. One day I fell from a very high rock, and broke my arm. For a long time I didn't know who I was."

"Now do you remember who you are?" asked Dr. Moore.

"Yes, I think I'll tell you." The young man whispered a name.

"You can't mean it!" cried Dr. Moore. "How strange! Who found you after you fell?"

"An old Indian found me, and took me to his hut. He took care of me, and got a doctor to fix my arm. I came here to Captain Daniel as soon as I remembered who I was."

"Why didn't you go right back to your home?" asked Dr. Moore.

"Because I wanted to be perfectly well before I went home. You see, I used to live with my uncle. It didn't seem right for me to go back home until I was sure that I was well again."

"I see," said Dr. Moore. "Come over some day to see me, and tell me some more. I will look at your arm then."

"It is almost well," said the young man.

"Good!" said Dr. Moore. "You are doing the right thing. You should stay here and help Captain Daniel. You will like the four children when you get to know them."

"I'm sure I shall," said the young man. "You won't tell anyone about me, will you?"

"No, I won't," promised the doctor. "I will say that you are Captain Daniel's old friend and a handy man. The children can call you Joe."

"Right!" said Joe. "My middle name is Joseph, anyway."

Dr. Moore and Captain Daniel went back to the barn, leaving the strange handy man still fixing the lobster pot.

"Do you feel better now, Captain?" asked the doctor.

"I should say so! Thanks for fixing it up."

"The stranger is all right, Mr. Alden," said Dr. Moore. "Joe is a very fine fellow, he's very handy, and Captain Daniel has known him all his life."

"You are sure then that everything is all right?" Mr. Alden asked sharply.

"Yes," said the doctor. "The children will like Joe."

"I want to go and see Joe," said Benny.

"Not now," cried Henry. "We haven't time. Don't you remember we are going back to the mainland and buy groceries and dishes?"

"Of course I remember!" said Benny. "I've been waiting and waiting."

Captain Daniel took them back to the mainland. The doctor and his mother left the others at the store.

"We had a wonderful time seeing your new home," said Mrs. Moore.

"May we come again?" asked Dr. Moore, with a twinkle in his eye.

"You know you may," said Jessie, smiling back. "Come any time after we get some dishes."

"Come on, Jessie," said Benny. "Let's buy things."

"Right," said Jessie. And they all went into the store. They walked straight to the piles of cooking dishes.

"We are going to get a lot of dishes," said Jessie. "May we have a big box first, so that we can put the things into it as we find them?"

"Certainly," said the girl. "How is this one? Is it big enough?"

"That's just fine," said Henry. "Look, Jessie, see

that big pail? We ought to have two, one for drinking water, and one for dishwater."

"That's a good idea," said Jessie. "I hope we won't forget anything."

Soon they had everything they wanted.

"It's four o'clock," said Henry. "Let's go up to the house and get our swimming suits and towels."

"And my bear," cried Benny.

"We will get your bear if we don't get anything else," said Jessie.

"I think we'll have to pack another box at the house," said Henry.

"Let's pack old clothes," said Jessie. "We certainly don't want to wear these school clothes."

"I should say not," said Henry. "We couldn't explore an island with good clothes on."

"Are we going to explore?" asked Benny.

"Yes, Benny," said Violet. "I'm going to take my paints and make pictures of things we find."

"Good!" cried Henry, who liked Violet's little pictures very much.

By this time they had come to the house. "Let's find what we want to take," said Henry, "and bring it to Jessie's room."

Mrs. McGregor, the housekeeper, met them at the door and said, "Jessie, don't you want to see what Mr. Alden has bought, before you pack your things?"

"Bought? Yes, indeed," replied Jessie.

Upstairs on Jessie's bed was a big pile of new play clothes. There were four pairs of brown shoes, too.

"Just think of Grandfather's getting all these!" cried Jessie. "Just what we need. Let's each put on one of these suits and not take any school clothes at all."

"I like my new shoes," said Benny. He sat down on the floor and began to take off his old shoes at once.

Mr. Alden smiled as he sat alone downstairs in his big chair and listened to the happy shouting.

"Now for the packing box," said Henry.

"Wait!" said Jessie. "Don't bring the box up here.

Each one of us can carry some things downstairs."

"I'll take the towels and my tools," said Henry.

"Violet and I will carry the workbag, paints, the swimming suits, and the other clothes," said Jessie. "Benny can bring the flashlight and the rest of the things."

They all went downstairs with their arms full.

"Now did we forget anything?" asked Jessie.

"We forgot my bear, I guess," said Benny, who had come downstairs again with a very funny-looking animal in his hand. He laid the bear beside the box.

"The most important thing of all!" cried Jessie, packing the bear carefully in the box.

"We're all ready to go, Grandfather," said Henry, when the bear was added to the box. "Are you sure you won't be lonesome?"

"Thank you, my boy. No indeed!" said Mr. Alden quickly. He knew the children would not go at all unless he were careful. "I wouldn't go with you if I could. I need a little rest without any children or dogs around."

The children did not need to look up to see the twinkle in his eye, for they knew very well that he liked to have them near him.

"You won't hear Watch bark at the milkman for a long time," said Benny.

"What shall I do, Benny?" asked his grandfather. "I shall miss the barking and noise in the morning."

"Good-by!" called everybody, as the car started. Mr. Alden and Mrs. McGregor waved until the car was out of sight.

"They're wonderful children," said Mrs. McGregor. "They are very clever. And yet they're never too busy to be kind to everybody. Even little Benny, now, didn't forget to say 'Good-by' to the cook."

"Thank you, Mrs. McGregor," said Mr. Alden. "That means a lot to me because you know them so well."

He smiled as he went back to his big chair. He wanted to think about the children as they went across the island and into their new home.

The children got out of the car at the dock.

"Don't you forget that bread and milk, Jessie!" said Benny.

"Oh, my!" cried Jessie. "We almost went over without a thing to eat. How lucky we are to have a store so near this dock. Let's get lots of bread and milk. If we have bread and milk, we can live without eating anything else."

"I have to have my vegetables," said Benny.

"Of course," said Jessie, laughing. "We'll have lots of other things."

"I want some supper now, Jessie," said Benny. "I don't want to hear any more talking about it."

Jessie laughed. "I'm glad you are so hungry,

Benny," she said. "I almost forgot to buy our supper. It's only six o'clock. We can have supper ready in an hour. Here comes Henry with the bread and milk."

"I can't wait an hour," said Benny. "I have to go to bed in an hour because Mrs. McGregor says so."

"Not tonight, Mr. Benny," said Henry, laughing.

Captain Daniel put the boxes into the boat and started the motor. In a very short time they came to the island, and Captain Daniel helped the children carry the boxes to the barn.

"Good luck!" said Captain Daniel, as he set down the last box. "I hope you will like your new home."

"Oh, we shall!" Jessie called after him. "And thank you. You have been so kind to us."

"Now!" said Henry. "Let's get to work."

"Oh, isn't this exciting!" cried Jessie. "You open the boxes and Benny and I will set up the table."

What a noise they made! Henry took off the cover of the box. The others pulled out the barrels and laid the wide board across them. Then the whole family unpacked the blue-and-white dishes.

"We'll wash four bowls and four spoons," said

Jessie. "We won't heat water to wash all the dishes tonight. It is lucky that Captain Daniel brought us a little water."

"No," said Violet, "we can't put things away until we have a dish cupboard."

"Tomorrow," laughed Henry, "I will make that dish cupboard the very first thing."

Violet piled the bread on a plate, while Jessie put two bottles of milk on the table. So with packing boxes for chairs, the four children sat down. They put the bread into the bowls and poured the cold milk over it. With their new spoons, they began to eat their first delicious supper in their new home.

"We must get something for Watch to eat," said Henry, as the dog ate two big slices of their bread.

"How many pieces of bread may I have, Jessie?" asked Benny.

"All you want!" cried both Jessie and Henry.

When supper was over, Jessie got up so suddenly that her chair went over. "Let's wash these dishes right away," she said, "and then make our beds."

So the children started for the spring, each with a bowl and spoon. They soon saw that the water from the spring came up into a barrel and ran over the top. The stream ran into the woods.

"We had better wash dishes in the stream because we may want to drink the water in the barrel," said Henry.

As he waited for the others, he thought he saw a vegetable garden on the other side of the house. He could not see very well because it was getting dark. "A funny thing to find on an island," he thought to himself.

"I'm going to bring down my own bed myself," said Benny, starting back to the barn. "I want the stall right next to Jessie's for my bedroom."

"He's sleepy," said Jessie, looking at her little watch. "It's eight o'clock, and I'm sleepy, too."

After all the children were in bed, Jessie sat up suddenly and listened. She heard a sleepy little voice saying over and over, "Jessie, I want my bear. I want my bear."

She got up at once. With the flashlight, she soon found the funny-looking animal in the packing box and took it to Benny.

When Jessie woke again, it was morning.

Chapter 3

The Garden

Jessie was not the first one to wake up the next day. At six o'clock, Henry went very quietly to her "room" and opened the swinging door to let Watch out. The dog came very quietly and followed Henry as he walked out of the barn to the spring. Henry stood still and looked around. He was right. It was just as he thought last night. There was a garden, with rows and rows of vegetables in it.

"I wonder if this garden belongs to Captain Daniel," thought Henry.

Then he heard a little noise, and turned around. A young man was coming toward him. His head was down as he walked. Henry looked at him carefully. Henry thought the man looked very sad, but he forgot that when the stranger looked up and smiled.

"I'm Joe," he said. "I'm the handy man. How do you like your garden?"

"Mine? Is it mine?" asked Henry.

"Yes. There are two gardens on this island. One belongs to Captain Daniel and this one is yours."

"How did that happen?" asked Henry. "I just got here."

"Well, your grandfather knew that you would rather plant it yourself. If you did, it would be too late to start planting when you got out of school. So he told Captain Daniel to plant it, and he said you would weed and look after the garden when you came."

"I will," said Henry, opening one of the peas. "These are big enough to eat now."

"Yes," said Joe. "The peas are just right, but nothing else will be ready until later."

"Haven't you ever eaten tiny vegetables? We did once," said Henry. "We pulled them because there were too many of them in the garden. It makes me hungry when I remember how good they were. The girls make such good things to eat out of almost nothing."

The other children appeared at just that minute.

But it was Benny who spoke first. "Hello, Joe," he said. "You look just like Joe. Is this your garden?"

"No," said Joe, laughing. "It's yours."

"Oh, no, it isn't," said Benny.

"It is ours, Benny," said Henry. "Joe and Captain Daniel started it for us, and you may help me weed it."

"Not now," said Benny. "I want my breakfast."

"We'll eat soon," said Jessie, smiling at Joe. "This is Violet, and I'm Jessie."

Joe said, "Yes, Captain Daniel told me all your names. I feel as if I knew you all."

"Oh, look," cried Benny. "Peas! I'd like peas for dinner!"

"Our dinner is all planned then," said Jessie. "We'll have peas, and everyone will help pick and shell them."

They walked slowly back to the barn, leaving Joe at the woodpile.

"He's nice, isn't he?" said Violet, as they walked along. They all agreed that he was.

After the four bowls and the bread and milk were set on the table, the children sat down carefully on the packing boxes. Then Jessie said, "I think that after breakfast we'd better make a plan for the summer. Every day we must go swimming, and every day we must cook something at noon. After dinner we must either make something or go exploring."

"Make something, such as a dish cupboard, I suppose," said Henry, looking at Violet.

"That's not a bad idea, Henry!" cried Violet.

"I will make you a cupboard this very day," said Henry.

"Let's wash the dishes and pick the peas now," said Jessie. "Henry can make the dish cupboard while we shell the peas. We'll take the dishpan to hold them."

On the way to the spring with their bowls and the dishpan, they passed Joe at the woodpile.

"Henry," called Joe, stopping his work, "did you know that Captain Daniel goes over to the mainland every morning for groceries? If you need any groceries, you may leave your order on a piece of paper in the box on the dock. Captain Daniel will bring your order back to the island before dinner."

"Oh, how nice," said Jessie. "I was wondering what to do about milk. Ours is almost gone."

"Just write what you want and I will take it down now," said Joe. "Here is my pen."

Jessie and Henry sat down facing each other on rocks to think.

"We must have butter for the peas," said Jessie, writing it down on a piece of paper from Joe's pocket.

"We want bread and four bottles of milk every day all summer," said Henry.

"Sugar," called Benny. "And some dog bread for Watch."

"Good!" said Henry. "I almost forgot Watch."

"I want to go with Joe and see the little box," said Benny, taking Joe's hand.

"Let him go," said Violet. "I'll wash his bowl for him, and we can pick peas without him."

Then the older children set to work. They picked enough for dinner, but lots of peas were left.

"Enough for two more dinners," said Henry, very pleased, "and more will grow. Now I will start that cupboard while you girls shell the peas.

"How many places will you need to put things, Jessie?"

"One shelf for spoons and things," said Jessie.

"And one shelf for dishes," said Violet.

"And one shelf for pans and kettles," said Jessie, "and an extra shelf for groceries."

The two girls sat in the open door of the barn shelling peas. Henry began to build the cupboard.

"What time shall we go swimming?" asked Jessie.

"We could go in right before lunch," said Henry. "Or if you were too busy cooking, we could swim before breakfast, and maybe again at four o'clock."

"Fine," said Jessie. "Before breakfast when we feel like it—four o'clock when we don't. Maybe both and go to bed at eight o'clock, or as soon as it gets dark."

"Oh, dear! Do we all have to go to bed so early?" asked Violet.

"You'll want to, believe me," said Henry. "You wait and see."

When the peas were shelled, Benny came running back. "It's a big box, Violet," he said, "and it has a little door, and it will hold lots of bottles of milk and everything. I like to open the door and take out the things."

"What did you take out?" asked Violet.

"Oh, Captain Daniel let me take out some letters and packages," answered Benny.

"Maybe you'd like to do that every day, Benny," said Henry. "You may take the order down to the box. Then you may get the groceries and letters when they come."

"I'd like to do that," said Benny. "Captain Daniel was there and he said he's bringing our groceries soon. Then I can open the little door and get them."

"That's fine," said Henry. He was glad to please Benny and get a little work done at the same time. "Come and hold this door for me, will you?"

"Oh, our cupboard has doors!" said Violet. She watched Henry put two pieces of heavy cloth on the doors so that they would open and shut.

The morning passed very quickly. Jessie lighted the little stove, boiled some water in the kettle, and put in the peas. When they were done, she added some salt, and filled four dishes with peas. On the top of each dish she put a piece of butter. There was no need to call anyone, for the whole family and the dog stood watching her.

"Oh, boy!" cried Henry, as he began to eat.

"Oh, boy!" cried Benny.

Violet said nothing, but when her first dish was empty she passed it for more.

"This is what I like," said Jessie. "Everything seems better when we have to work to get it."

It was fun to put white paper in the new dish cupboard and find the best places for each cup and bowl. And at one o'clock the barn was once more in order, the cupboard was shut, and the four children and their dog were ready to explore the island.

Chapter 4

Clamming

The children walked through the beach grass and sat on the sand.

"Jessie, look at that!" cried Benny, pointing. As he spoke, a stream of water shot out of the sand. But Henry did not stop to say how pretty it was. "Clams!" he shouted. He jumped up and took a stick from the beach. The rest of the children and the dog ran to watch Henry as he began to dig. Sure enough, he took a real clam from the wet hole.

"Oh, I wish I had a shovel!" cried Henry. "There are lots of clams here. See that hole, and that!"

"Let's run up and get two big spoons and the dishpan," cried Jessie. They raced for the tools, leaving Benny and Violet with the stick. When they came running back, they found that Benny had dug out another clam.

"I am going to keep mine," said Benny, very pleased with himself. "It is such a pretty purple color."

"You can put all yours together into this pan, Benny," said Jessie, giving him a saucepan. "You won't want to keep them when you find out how good they are to eat."

The children took off their shoes and set to work.

"There's another!" cried Benny. "I can't dig fast enough."

Watch seemed to know what was going on. He stood still a minute watching Benny dig with the stick. Then he began to dig too, with his paws.

"Good old Watch!" cried Benny. "You can do all my digging if you want, and I will take the clams out for you." As if he really did understand, the dog waited for Benny to show him where the clam was. Then he began to dig again. The older children

laughed to see the sand fly under his paws, but they were very glad to see the pan fill up.

"I suppose these are for dinner tomorrow," said Henry, as he threw a clam on the pile.

"Yes," said Jessie. "These will keep all right here. We can cover them all over with seaweed."

"I think we have enough," said Henry, looking at the pan. He went to the water and pulled out a lot of wet seaweed. He spread this carefully over the clams.

"I wish we knew what was around that next point," he said. "Let's find out."

"We're exploring now, Benny," said Violet. "You must keep your eyes open."

Benny's eyes were certainly open when he went around the point. In the water near the beach was a little raft.

"Oh, I know that Grandfather fixed this place for us to swim in!" said Benny.

"Of course he did," said Henry. "The water here can't be over my head, but it is deep enough for swimming."

The children explored until three o'clock. Then they all agreed to go swimming, and went to their rooms to put on their suits. When they came back to the beach, they all walked together into the water.

"Cold!" said Benny, walking out again. "I like warm water."

"That's because you're not in all over," said Jessie, laughing. "You just watch Henry, and you'll soon like it."

They all watched Henry as he went quickly into the water and began swimming hand over hand to the raft. Watch swam along beside him.

"It's great!" Henry shouted, as he sat on the raft "Come on out, Jessie."

"I will, just as soon as I get Benny in," she called back. "You'll never be warm unless you go in all over, Benny." But Benny would not go in. He sat in his swimming suit, throwing stones into the water. Violet was down the beach, looking for seaweed. She said she would stay with Benny while Jessie swam out to the raft. As Jessie and Henry sat with their feet in the water, they saw a man coming.

"It's Joe!" said Henry. It was Joe, and he was wearing a swimming suit.

Henry watched as Joe came along the beach and sat down beside Benny.

"How is the water today?" asked Joe.

"It's awfully cold," replied Benny. "It's ice melted."

"I guess that's because you haven't been in all over," said Joe, smiling.

"Yes, that's what Jessie says," said Benny.

"That is called rockweed," said Joe suddenly, as Violet picked up a long piece of brown seaweed.

"There are beautiful seaweeds around here. See this dark green one on the sand? And here's another red one. Look! There is a piece of it in that wave!" Joe went into the water, and Violet followed him.

"Oh, there it goes!" she cried. "We've lost it."

Benny was standing up by this time, looking into the waves. He did not even feel the water washing over his feet. The seaweed came up on a wave and went down again. This time Benny went after it.

"I've got it!" he shouted. He was right. He had caught the red seaweed, and he was wet all over.

"Good for you, Benny!" said Joe with a smile. "Let me take it a minute."

"Here," said Benny, handing the seaweed to Joe. He did not know that he was standing in melted ice.

"Say, I have an idea," said Joe. "Float the seaweed like this in water. Then pick it up by putting a piece of writing paper under it and spread out the feathery branches with a pin."

"Will the seaweed stay on the paper?" asked Violet.

"Yes," said Joe. "There is something in the seaweed that makes it stick to the paper when it is dry. Then you can use the paper for writing letters."

"Oh, I'd like that," cried Violet, "but I'd also like to make a seaweed collection!"

"Fine!" said Henry, for he and Jessie had come back from the raft to see what was going on. "You can write down the names of the seaweed and make a little book."

"That will be hard to do. There aren't many everyday names for seaweed," said Joe.

"You know lots of things, don't you, Joe?" said Benny.

The three older children agreed, for they had seen how clever Joe had been in getting Benny into the cold water without his knowing it.

After they had dressed and were sitting down to supper, Henry was thinking about Joe. Later, when he was in bed, he thought, "Joe is a very strange handy man, to know the names of the different kinds of seaweed."

Chapter 5

Summer Plan

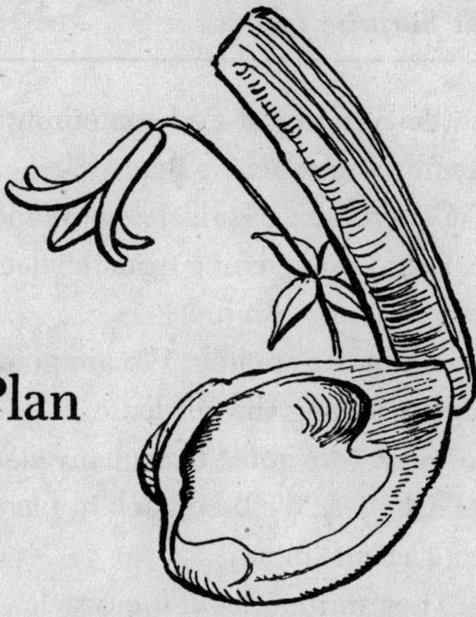

"We must go on exploring the island," said Henry, the morning after the clam digging. "It may rain any day and the days are just flying by."

"We can go this morning," said Jessie, coming to the doorway of the barn. "The clams will not take very long to cook, and that's all we are going to have for dinner except, of course, bread, butter, and milk. If we get back by eleven o'clock, we shall have plenty of time."

"It's settled, then," said Henry. "Let's take the big

kettle. We might find something we want to bring home. Now where is Benny?"

"There he is," said Jessie, pointing.

Benny was coming from the dock. He had a basket of groceries with him.

"Hurry up, Benny. We are going to explore," said Henry, taking the kettle.

"Aren't we going to cook my clams?" asked Benny.

"Oh, yes. We'll be back in plenty of time to cook your clams, Benny."

They started down the beach.

"See this funny shell," said Jessie. She dug it out with her foot. "It is just like a little boat. Let's save it." She dropped it into the kettle.

"And here's a beautiful one," said Violet. "Let's save all the shells we find."

"Look at this pretty purple flower, Jessie, right in the sand," said Benny.

"Let's save all the flowers we find, too," said Jessie. "Put it in the kettle, Benny."

Just then Henry began to jump around on the sand. The others watched him in surprise.

"What in the world is the matter with you?" asked Jessie, as Watch began to jump with him.

"I have a great idea! Oh, boy!" cried Henry.

"Tell us," said Violet, as they all sat down on the sand.

"Well," began Henry, "you all know what a museum is—"

"I don't," said Benny.

"Oh, sure you do, Benny," cried Henry. "You must

have seen pictures of museums; places where they keep all kinds of birds and animals and flowers."

"And shells," said Violet.

"That's it," cried Henry, looking at his sister. "You know what my idea is already, don't you?"

"I think so," said Violet. "And I think it is a perfectly wonderful idea."

"Oh, do you?" asked Henry. "I wasn't sure."

"What is this idea?" asked Jessie.

"Well," answered Henry, "we are sure to find some interesting things on this island to keep. We found these things without looking at all. Maybe we shall find lots more—butterflies, birds, seaweed—"

"We could clean out the upstairs in the barn," said Jessie.

"And have a museum," said Benny.

"I can't think of anything I'd rather do!" said Jessie. "That will give us lots of things to do on rainy days. Violet could make little signs for everything, and you could make a table to go around the room. And I will dry the flowers between newspapers and put the shells in boxes."

"We wouldn't have real birds, would we?" asked Violet, looking worried.

"Oh, no!" cried Henry. "We could cut birds out of heavy paper and color them—every bird we see."

"Then we could cut down some small trees and put the birds on the branches," said Jessie. "I've seen them in the museum."

"Good!" said Henry. "We might find old birds' nests to put up in the trees. We will have plenty of fun this whole summer."

Violet began to write down in the little book:

1. Birds
2. Flowers
3. Seaweed
4. Shells
5. Butterflies

"That's enough for a beginning," said Henry, standing up. "We shall have to be on the watch every minute."

And so the exploring party set out once more, looking at the trees for birds, and dropping flowers and shells into the kettle.

"How can I write the names of these shells when we don't know their names?" asked Violet. She dropped a long, thin clam shell into the kettle, but nobody knew what it was.

"I suppose we could get a book about shells from the library," said Henry. "Grandfather said we could go across to the mainland with Captain Daniel if we wanted to, but I don't want to leave this island for even a minute."

"Something will turn up," said Jessie.

Something did turn up. The very minute the explorers came back to their barn, they saw Joe getting into the motorboat.

"Oh, *wait!*" called Jessie, running down to the dock.

"Don't hurry," called Joe. "Plenty of time."

But all the children kept on running just the same.

"Are you going to the stores now, Joe?" asked Jessie.

"That's just where I am going," replied Joe. "I will get anything you want and I shall be back in an hour."

"Then you will go right by the library!" cried Jessie. "Would you be willing to get us some books?"

"Yes, I can get all the books you want by signing for them," he said.

Joe took out a pen and a piece of paper and gave them to Jessie. "Write the names of the books you want and I will get them."

"I can't," answered Jessie, giving back the paper. "We don't know the names of the books. But we want books with pictures in them to tell us the names of flowers, birds, shells, butterflies, and seaweed."

Joe smiled in a queer way and said, "I could ask the girl in the library to pick them out for you."

"That's right," agreed Henry. "She would know."

But when Joe went into the library, he did not ask for any help. He gave the girl in the library the names of so many books that she had to write very fast. Then a small boy went off to get them. When the books were tied up, the strange handy man went away, leaving the girl and small boy looking after him in surprise.

Joe was really delighted to go over to the barn and see the children. He knocked at their open door with his foot, as his arms were full of books.

"Oh, come in!" cried Jessie. She put a cover on the kettle and came over to him at once. "Did you have any luck?"

"I don't know. I hope so," said Joe.

"Oh, Henry," cried Jessie, "I don't know what to do first, but I suppose I must fix the clams."

"You surely must," said Henry. "We are so hungry we could eat the chairs, but I will not open the books until after we eat."

"Won't you stay to dinner, Joe?" asked Jessie. "I washed the clams six times and they are cooking now. I think they are almost done."

Oh, how Joe wanted to stay to dinner! "I-I—" he said.

"That's fine!" said Jessie, as if he had said 'Yes.' "

"You're our first guest," shouted Benny with delight. "But you'll have to wash your own dishes."

"Oh no, he won't, Benny," cried Jessie. "You shouldn't say such things."

"I would like to wash my own dishes," said Joe, smiling. "And I really would like to see if the books are all right."

Violet smiled, because the smell of the clams was good enough to make anyone hungry. While Jessie melted some butter, Violet went out and brought back five of Benny's purple flowers and put one at each place.

The clams were all open when Jessie looked in the kettle. She began to take them out with a saucepan.

"Please let me do that," said Joe. "That kettle is so heavy."

"Thank you so much," said Jessie. "I can put the melted butter into the cups." She did this quickly, and then poured the clam water into five bowls. Violet set them all on the table.

"Oh, dear, what shall we do for another place to sit?" asked Jessie.

"Let me bring the block from my woodpile," said Joe.

When Joe came back with the block of wood, Benny asked, "How do you eat clams, anyway?"

"Pull the clam out," said Joe. "See! Then put him into the clam water, then into the melted butter—"

"Then you put him into your mouth," said Benny.

They all laughed at Benny, but they did not talk much, for they were too busy eating. Joe picked out Benny's clams for him.

"I never had so much fun at a dinner in my life," said Joe when the clams were gone, "but I want to help with the dishes."

"All right," said Jessie. "I put the kettle of water on to heat before we sat down. You may wipe dishes if you really want to."

When the dishwater was hot, the dishes were washed and soon were all put away in the cupboard.

Then Jessie said, "Now show us the books, Joe!"

Chapter 6

The Museum

Joe and the children sat around the table to look at the books. Henry took off the paper and found twelve interesting-looking books.

"The Butterfly Book," said Jessie.

"The Shell Book," said Violet.

"The Flower Book," said Henry. "Oh, these three books must belong to a set. Just look at the beautiful pictures."

The handy man seemed to be just as interested as the children. He soon found a picture of the purple flower on the table. It was the Beach Pea. Then Joe showed the children the names of the shells they had found. He saw that Henry was staring at him. "How did you ever learn all this?" asked Henry.

"Oh, I just picked it up," said Joe. "I used to live near the beach."

Joe saw that he would have to be more careful, because it appeared that he knew too much for a handy man. And so he said he would have to get back to his work.

After Joe had gone, Henry said, "Let's look upstairs." He ran up the stairs and the others followed with the dog. First Henry opened the big windows. Then he looked around the room. The pile of straw was at one end. In the corner stood an old straight-backed chair. Jessie went over and shook it.

"Wonderful!" said Jessie. "We'll use that when Grandfather comes to call. To think of having a real guest chair!"

"I wish we had some boards," said Henry. "I thought we might find some up here."

"What is this?" asked Benny.

"Boards!" shouted Henry.

Some eight-foot boards were piled on the floor under the straw.

"Well, now," cried Henry, "how lucky we are! I'll get right to work. I can carry the boards down under the trees, and saw them to make tables."

"I ought to dry the flowers," said Jessie. "Violet can look up their names and Benny can help carry down the boards."

"We ought to have lots of newspapers for drying the flowers," said Violet, going downstairs. "And we haven't a single newspaper."

"Joe has," said Benny to everyone's surprise. "He gets two every day, so he must have a lot."

"You go ask him, Benny, will you?" said Violet. "Just ask him for old ones, and be sure to thank Joe."

When Benny arrived at Captain Daniel's hut, he knocked at the door.

"Hello!" called a voice. Benny walked around to the other side of the hut. Joe and the captain sat there cleaning fish.

"Have you any old newspapers?" asked Benny. "Not to read, but to dry flowers between."

"We certainly have," said Joe, smiling. He pointed to some piles of old newspapers.

"Oh, one pile will be enough," cried Benny, delighted. "Jessie only wanted a dozen. Thank you, Joe. She will be surprised."

Jessie was surprised and pleased.

"Have you a thin board about a foot long?" she called to Henry.

"How's this?" asked Henry.

"Perfect. Go get it, Benny," said Jessie.

But she had used the wrong words for Benny and the right words for Watch. When the dog heard "Go get it," he ran out of the barn to Henry who put the board carefully in the dog's mouth. Then Watch ran back and laid the board at Jessie's feet. Jessie was so pleased that she stopped her work and gave him a piece of bread.

The girls smoothed the flowers out on the newspapers, just as they had done in school. Then they covered the flowers with more papers and a board and put a large stone on top.

"I hear a motorboat," said Henry.

"I'm going down to see," said Benny. "There might be something for us."

Jessie said, "Don't be too sure." To her surprise he came back in a few minutes with a big box.

"We did get something!" he cried. "It's from Grandfather! Captain Daniel said so."

Henry opened the big box.

"Sweaters!" he said.

Benny took his at once. "I know mine is that red one," he said. "And I guess that purple one is Violet's."

There was a beautiful blue one for Jessie, and a brown one for Henry. They all put them on to see how they looked.

"Grandfather thinks it's going to get cold," said Jessie.

"So do I," answered Henry. "I think we shall be glad of these presents very soon."

When Jessie woke up late that night she heard rain falling on the roof of the barn. She put on her

shoes and shut all the windows. Henry got up to help shut the barn door. "Now I guess we'll keep dry," he whispered.

"The rain is coming in somewhere," said Jessie softly. They listened, and they could hear the sound of water dropping near the stove.

"We mustn't let the stove get wet," cried Henry, speaking out loud. "Get the big kettle!"

Henry put it under the stream of water. The water seemed to come faster and faster into the kettle.

"We can't go to sleep because the kettle might run over," said Henry after a minute.

"What's the matter, Jessie?" called Benny in a sleepy voice.

"Rain is coming through the roof," said Henry. "You go back to sleep."

"I can't," cried Benny. "Rain is coming in my window, too, and all over me."

"Oh, dear!" cried Jessie. "Where is the flashlight?"

With the flashlight, the two older children soon saw that the wall near Benny's bed was very wet. A stream of water was running in under his window.

"Get up, Benny!" cried Henry.

Benny came out slowly. "I don't like this bed," he said. He began to cry. "I like my bed at Grandfather's house, and I want to go home! It's nice and dry there."

"Now, Benny, don't be like that!" cried Jessie. "You're a big boy, and you ought to be up helping us. You wouldn't like it if we left you at home, would you?"

"No," said Benny. This idea woke him up, and he started to help move his bed out.

"What's the matter?" called Violet.

"It's raining in this barn!" said Benny. "Maybe on you, too."

"No, it's not," said Violet. "But I can hear it coming in somewhere."

"It's coming in all over the place," cried Henry.

"I wish we had more kettles," said Jessie. "I'll put one pail under this window and the other pail in the corner."

"We can't go to sleep," said Violet. "The pails and kettle will run over."

"The rest of you can go to sleep," said Henry. "I will stay up and empty the pails. Benny, you get into my bed. I think we have found all the places where the rain is coming in."

Benny was glad to get into bed and he was soon asleep again. Henry sat up for an hour. He emptied the pails once more, and then crawled in beside Benny. The rain had almost stopped.

"I'll fix the roof tomorrow," he thought. "And maybe Joe will help me. He's a very handy man."

The next morning it was still raining. The children dressed and ate breakfast and then watched the rain.

"One of us must go outside for the groceries," said

Henry, "and I think I'm the one. My clothes are going to get awfully wet, so what shall I do while they dry?"

"Where are all your other clothes?" asked Benny.

Henry pointed to the clothesline over the stove.

"They aren't dry yet," said Jessie. "I'm sorry now that I washed them."

"Henry can go to bed while his clothes dry," said Benny.

"Say, listen, Benny!" cried Henry. "How would you like to go to bed? You get busy and think of something I could put on."

"Jessie could make you a suit out of a blanket," said Benny suddenly.

"I really could!" cried Jessie. "It's lucky we brought along Violet's workbag. I'll make you a pair of pants out of a blanket. And you can put on your new sweater while your things dry."

"Good for you, Jessie," said Henry. "Now let's be sure we have thought of everything we want, so I won't have to go out again."

"I have an idea," said Benny. "Why don't you put on your swimming suit to go outside and then your clothes won't get wet?"

"That is a good idea, Benny. What would we do without you?" said Henry.

"Benny, you are wonderful," agreed Jessie.

Benny laughed and said, "I know you could make pants out of a blanket if you had to."

"I'll put on my swimming suit," said Henry. "You be thinking of what you want."

Jessie said, "There will be some potatoes in the box because I ordered them. And all that bread and milk. Do you think you can carry it all? I am going to make some clam chowder, and I'll need onions from the garden. The onions aren't very big, but big enough."

"I'll get the onions first," said Henry, appearing in his swimming suit, "and give them to you through the door. I think I can carry everything else."

Henry handed the little onions to Jessie through the partly open door. When he came in with the basket of groceries, he looked as if he had been swimming.

After a rub down with a towel, Henry put on his dry clothes and was ready for work.

"This is a perfect day to work on our museum things," he said. "I can make some boxes for the shells and butterflies."

Soon the table was covered with wood, paper, paints, and tools.

At half-past eleven, Jessie stopped her work to make the chowder.

"I'm going to use these little onions for the chowder," she said.

Jessie melted some butter and put the onions in it. Then she added water and salt and the sliced potatoes. When the potatoes were done, she added the cut-up clams and at the very last minute, the milk.

Soon, when dinner was ready, the four children took their bowls of chowder and sat down, not minding the rain at all.

"Jessie, you can make *anything!*" cried Henry.

"Yum, yum! Jessie can make good chowder!" said Benny.

After dinner, the children painted birds and fixed the feathery seaweed for their museum. Henry went upstairs to put up the tables.

By the time it was dark, the Alden Museum was very well started.

"I think the birds are the best thing in the museum," said Benny. But Benny did not know what they were to find the next day.

Chapter 7

Exploring

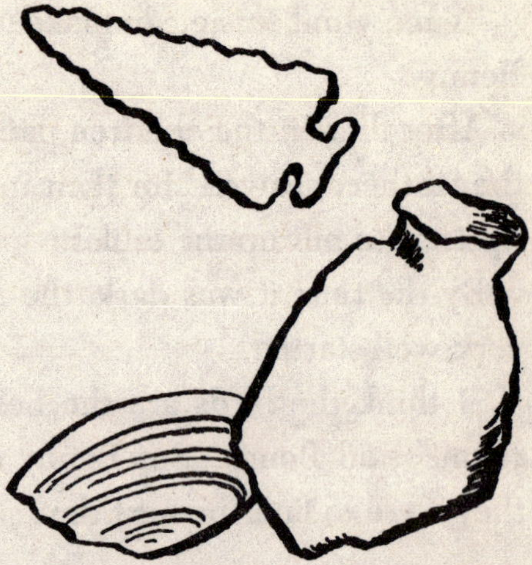

The next morning the rain had stopped, and it was a beautiful day. First, the four children went swimming. Then, after breakfast they started out with the big kettle to explore again.

"Let's go down to the very end of the island today," said Henry.

"I'll make a picture of the island as we go along," said Violet, taking the blue book.

They walked along slowly until they could see the very end of the island.

"Look, oh, look!" cried Jessie. "What a big pile of shells!"

"It's taller than Benny," cried Henry, as he and the others ran to the shell-pile.

"They're all broke," said Benny, picking up some shells.

"Broken, Benny," said Henry.

"Well, broken, then," said Benny. "Old broken clam shells. No pretty ones for our museum."

"Yes, but look!" said Jessie. "They are all clam shells, just as if somebody had sat here for years and years getting out clams."

"Maybe they did," said Violet.

"Who did?" asked Benny.

"I don't know, Benny," replied Henry. "I know I never saw anything like it before, not even in a picture." He took a stick and dug in the pile.

Violet made a little picture in her book of the shell-pile. Then the children started to explore the other side of the island. They found that this side of the island was very rocky. Jessie, Henry, and Violet

were looking up at the high rocks when Benny said suddenly, "Look, a little cave! Let's go in."

"He's right," said Henry, looking in.

"Come on, like this," said Benny, going in on his hands and knees.

The other children went after Benny, laughing. "Oh, it's just like a little room," cried Jessie. "And I can see another one."

"Nice in here," said Henry, looking around him. "Let's go on."

They all crawled after Henry and came to another little room. They could still see the ocean, as they looked back.

The children sat down, and Henry began to dig with the stick, just for fun. Suddenly he dug out a small stone.

"Oops!" cried Henry. "What is this?" He picked up the stone and rubbed off the wet sand. Then he jumped up.

"It's an Indian arrowhead!" he cried. "What do you know!"

"Let me see it," said Jessie. "It certainly is an arrowhead. See the little place at the end where they tied it to a stick?"

"They put feathers on the other end," said Henry.

"It's for our museum," cried Benny.

"So it is!" cried Henry. "You think of everything, Benny. Let's dig and see if we can find another. If Indians lived here, they had more than one arrow."

The children began to dig. When Watch saw what they were doing, he began to dig, too.

"If we find a lot of Indian things," cried Henry, "maybe some real museum will buy them."

"That is a good idea. Let's come here early some

morning and dig," said Jessie. "Besides, it's lots of fun."

Suddenly Watch stopped digging and began to bark.

"What's the matter, old boy? What are you trying to tell us?" asked Henry. He went over and put his hand in the hole Watch had dug and took out a big smooth stone.

"I think this is an old ax-head!" he cried, turning it over and over.

The other children came to look, and Benny took it in his hand. Watch barked again, sharply. Then he threw back his head and gave one long howl.

"Something is wrong," cried Henry. "Watch never howls."

"Oh, look, Henry!" cried Jessie in a frightened voice.

They all looked at the door and water was coming in almost at their feet.

"Let's get out of here!" shouted Henry, starting for the door. "Come just as fast as you can!"

They crawled as fast as they could, but the water was quite deep. Watch began to swim.

"Joe doesn't know where we are!" cried Benny. "Or he would save us. I'm scared."

"Don't talk, Benny. Keep going."

Soon they were in the first room.

"A wave is coming!" Henry shouted. "When it comes, get out fast!"

The wave came up and broke over them. Jessie caught Benny's arm and pulled him out. The four frightened children crawled through the water, and scrambled along the rocky edge before another wave came in. They rested there a short time and then crawled to the shell-pile.

"Be careful!" said Henry. "Don't fall."

"Oh, thank goodness!" cried Jessie, as they came to the dry sand.

"I'm all tired," said Benny crossly. "And I'm scared of that old cave."

"Well," said Henry, "I am the one who ought to have watched the tide. That cave is perfectly safe when the tide is out. Just think! How lucky we are to be out!"

"W-w-we-did-get-out," said Violet. "Th-th-thank-good-old-Watch-for-that." She was still so frightened that she shook all over.

"Right," said Henry. "Let's rest a little while. Then we'll go back the way we came."

When the family came walking slowly back to their barn, Joe saw that something was wrong. He waved to them from the hut.

"All right?" he called.

"No!" shouted Benny. "We're scared and almost dead! The water came in the cave almost all over us."

"What do you mean?" asked Joe. He was very excited.

"We crawled into a cave, and the tide came up and almost caught us, Joe," said Henry. "I should have looked for the tide. If Watch hadn't barked, we wouldn't have seen the waves coming in."

"I can see that you are all worn out," said Joe.

"You are too tired to get dinner. Captain Daniel has just made a big kettle of stew. Why don't you each bring a bowl down here and eat with us?"

Jessie looked at Joe and smiled. "We will," she said. "We'll each get a bowl and a spoon and we'll be right back."

When the children sat down on the sand by the little hut, they began to feel better. The hot stew was good. Benny looked sleepy.

"Where was this cave?" asked Joe.

"On the very end of the island," said Jessie. "We found some Indian things in it."

"What did you find?" asked Joe quickly.

Henry took the arrowhead out of his pocket and gave it to him.

"We found something else, too, but we forgot to bring it," he said.

"No, I brought it," said Benny, almost asleep. "It's in my pocket, and I can't get it out."

Joe put his hand in Benny's pocket, and pulled out the stone.

"An Indian ax-head!" Joe said at once.

"I thought it was," said Henry. "But you seem to be sure."

"Well, I guess I am sure," said Joe, turning it over. "Maybe there are other things in the cave."

"I'm scared to go in that old cave again," said Benny crossly.

"Oh, don't say that!" cried Joe. "Just watch the tide. There must be some good Indian digging in there. If you ever want company, I could go with you."

"Oh, would you?" said Henry. "Then we certainly would be all right. There is a big pile of shells near the cave, too."

"What! A shell-pile?" shouted Joe. "Then I will certainly go with you. I must!"

"Why?" asked Benny. "Why must you?" But it was the last word he spoke. He was fast asleep.

Joe was saved from answering Benny. He just smiled and said, "I'll carry him home for you. It will be the best thing for all of you to get some sleep."

Joe picked Benny up and took him to his own bed. Jessie, Violet, and Henry followed them to the barn. In a few minutes the other three children fell asleep right in the middle of the day.

Chapter 8

Indian Point

After a long sleep, the children were as good as new.

"I feel just like starting out again," said Jessie.

"So do I," agreed Henry. "I wonder why Joe was so excited over the shell-pile. Let's ask him.

"Why did you say you must see that pile of shells?" began Henry when they had found Joe at the hut.

"Because I'm interested in things like that," answered Joe. "A shell-pile means that Indians must have been on this island."

"Come right along, Joe," said Benny. "I'll show

it to you." He took hold of Joe's hand and tried to pull him up. The children laughed as Joe got on his feet. In a little while the explorers arrived at the shell-pile.

"What a wonderful thing to find!" shouted Joe.

"Why?" asked Jessie.

Joe was looking at some of the broken shells. "Well," he said, "I'm sure the Indians made this pile. Do you remember from school that they made shell money called wampum? Sometimes they used these quahog shells for the purple part. Quahogs are clams!"

"You think they sat here to make wampum?" asked Henry.

"Yes, and I think they dried clams here, too," replied Joe, looking at some unbroken quahog shells.

"Why?" asked Jessie.

Joe laughed and said, "These are whole clam shells, so the Indians must have sat here to take the clams out of the shells. They used to dry the clams and then eat them later."

"Jessie knew that," said Benny. "She said they sat here for years and years."

"But I didn't know they were Indians," said Jessie.

"Do you think we could find any wampum here, Joe?" asked Henry.

"No, I don't really. They would save it because it was money, but we might find some old tools they used. The Indians used to smooth the shells on stones, and then make the holes with tools they got from white men."

"Let's dig," said Benny. "You can tell us if we find a tool."

"I'd like to dig," said Joe. "But we ought to have something good to dig with. Let's go back and get something from Captain Daniel."

"I'm too tired," said Benny. "And so is Watch."

Henry laughed. "You sit right down with Watch and Violet," he said, "and don't go away from here, and don't get into trouble. The rest of us will get the things and come right back. Remember now!"

"All right," said Benny, sitting down.

"While you are waiting, you could do some digging with a stick," called Joe. "Save everything you aren't sure about."

Violet began at once to look over the broken shells. "Why don't you look, Benny?" she said. "Wouldn't it be wonderful if you and I found something good while they are gone? Let's try."

"You try," said Benny. "I don't care. All I can find is this big chicken leg."

"Chicken leg!" cried Violet. "That is too big for a chicken."

"Well, maybe a horse then. It's an old bone, anyway," said Benny. "I'll save it for Joe. He will know for sure."

Violet dug at the shells. "Benny, you know all these shells look as if someone broke them. And a lot of the purple part is gone. That means that Joe is right, and they did make wampum here."

"Of course Joe is right," said Benny. "Joe is always right."

"It seems funny to me," said Violet, "that Joe is

just a handy man. I shouldn't think he would be working here on this island if he knows so much."

"Maybe he does something else, too," said Benny. "And maybe he came here to have a good time and learn things this summer, just like us."

Then the others came back. They had clam hooks and a shovel, and Joe had a camera.

"A camera!" cried Benny. "You can take a picture of Watch digging up an Indian!"

"I wish I could," said Joe, laughing. "I want to take a picture of the shell-pile. You and Watch sit right where you are. That will show how big the shell-pile is."

Violet scrambled out of the way.

"No, no," said Joe. "Don't go. I want you in the picture, too. You stand beside Watch."

So Violet stood where she was, and Joe took the picture. He took four pictures, one from each side.

"Why do you want all these pictures, Joe?" asked Henry.

"Maybe I'd better tell you something," said Joe.

"If the people on the mainland knew about this pile, they would be over here with cameras and shovels before we could stop them. You wouldn't like that, would you?"

"Oh, no!" cried Benny. "We don't want a lot of people over here."

"You children had better not tell anyone about this shell-pile before your grandfather knows," said Joe.

"All right, we won't," said Henry. "We'll tell Grandfather when he comes to visit us. Now, let's dig. I'd like to do this for a living, Joe——go to far-off places and dig up old bones and things."

"Good for you, Henry!" cried Joe. "It is very interesting work, but let me warn you, it isn't all fun. You may work for a year and not find anything."

"Just like fishing," said Benny.

"Exactly," agreed Joe. "Maybe you'd like to work with Henry."

"No, I wouldn't," said Benny. "I'd rather fish, because you can eat the fish."

"You will help us now, won't you?" asked Henry. "We need every man we can get."

"Sure," said Benny. "Watch, you can help, too."

Watch obeyed, but he soon barked and held up his paw. There was a white bone sticking in it.

"A fishhook!" cried Joe. "Right in your paw, Watch! Here, let me take it out. It's a fishhook made from an animal bone."

"That means Indians used to fish here, doesn't it?" asked Henry.

"Yes, I think so," said Joe. "Now, do you want to work just a little more? I'd like to dig under the pile before we go."

"Sure," said Benny. "We're not hungry, because we ate so much stew. What do you think we'll find, Joe?"

"I haven't any idea," said Joe. He took the shovel and soon dug quite a big hole. They all got down on their hands and knees to look in the hole.

"Is that anything?" asked Violet, pointing. "It looks like a piece of a dish."

"It's a piece of a dish!" shouted Joe.

"Here is another piece!" said Jessie, handing it to Joe.

"I think that these are all pieces of a bowl," cried Joe. The children found some more pieces and gave them to Joe. He wiped off the sand and put the pieces together. "Yes, this is a cooking bowl," said Joe. "I'm sure now that Indians lived here. We know now that they used to get clams here, and that they made wampum here. We may find more things. This island is a wonderful place."

Violet could see that Joe kept his eyes on the bowl every minute.

"That dish tells us more than anything else we have found," said Joe.

"I don't think so," said Benny, to everyone's surprise. "I think my horse bone tells the most, because it tells that the Indians had horses. See!" Benny pointed to the bone sticking up out of the sand.

"Benny Alden," Joe almost shouted. "The Indians didn't have horses before the white man came. *Where* did you find this?"

"On the back of the pile," answered Benny. "We're digging on the wrong side, I guess."

"It's a man's bone, Benny!" cried Joe. "It's part of a skeleton. Do you know what a skeleton is?"

"Oh, yes," said Benny. "All of us have a skeleton inside us. It's made of bones."

"That's right," said Henry. "Show us exactly where you found the bone."

"Right here," said Benny, going to the other side of the pile.

"Let's dig!" cried Joe. "But be careful! Down, Watch! You're a good dog, but this is no place for you to dig. Oh, children, look!"

Another bone came in sight.

"If you don't mind, please let me do the digging, will you? Just sit and watch me."

The children sat back and watched Joe as he slowly dug the sand away. Even Benny was excited, as he saw twelve small bones side by side in the sand.

"There ought to be another set just like these," said Joe.

"There they are!" shouted Henry. "And look, Joe! Look at the arrowhead sticking out!"

"He was shot," cried Joe. "Shot with an arrow. This is the skeleton of an Indian!"

Before long the whole skeleton lay before the excited children.

"Well, well!" said Joe, sitting back to rest. "We can't move this skeleton because we haven't the right tools. It will be safe because nobody knows it is here. Let's cover him up again."

"Cover him up?" shouted Benny. "But we just found him, Joe! He is for our museum!"

"I know, Benny," answered Joe. "Will you leave him here, just to please me? We can dig some other day in the cave. Aren't you getting hungry now?"

"Yes, I am," said Benny. "Let's go home and get some bread and milk."

Jessie smiled at Joe. It was so easy to please Benny sometimes. "Shall we take the bowl, Joe?" she asked.

"Oh, yes! Take all the small things to put in your museum."

So the explorers took their collection of clam hooks and Indian things and started home for supper.

"Let's call this end of the island 'Indian Point,'" said Henry.

And that is what it was always called after that.

Chapter 9

A New Violin

After supper, a few days later, the children sat resting in the doorway of the barn.

"Listen!" said Violet suddenly.

Since Violet never said anything suddenly, everyone looked at her in surprise and listened. Then they heard the sound of a violin.

"Who can that be?" asked Violet.

"Let's find out," said Henry.

Watch ran right to Captain Daniel's hut and the four children followed. There sat Joe in the doorway, playing a real violin. He did not stop when he saw the children. They stared at him and watched his fingers fly as he played a very fast piece. When Joe finished, Benny said, "I didn't know you had a violin."

"Oh, *please* play it again! When did you learn to play?" cried Violet. "Could I hold it just a minute?"

Jessie and Henry were too surprised to speak. This was not at all like Violet. When Joe handed the violin to her, Violet took it and put it under her chin.

"Play something," said Joe.

"Oh, I can't play it," said Violet. "I'd just like to hold it a minute under my chin. Do you mind, Joe?"

"No! No!" said Joe, "but don't you want me to show you how to play it?"

"Not now," said Violet. "You play some more."

She gave the violin back as if she had played one all her life. Joe did play some more, first a slow little piece, and then a faster one.

But Jessie and Henry were not watching Joe. They were watching Violet. She stood without moving all the time Joe was playing.

Joe was watching Violet, too. He was sure she could learn to play well, because she seemed to like the violin so much.

When the family went back to the barn at last, they were all thinking of Joe's wonderful playing. That night, when Jessie went to sleep, it seemed to her that Joe played such a sad piece that Violet cried. But when Jessie woke up, she knew that it was real crying that she heard, for Violet was crying softly. Jessie got up at once.

"What is the matter?" she asked, falling on her knees beside Violet's bed. "Why are you crying?"

"I-I w-want to learn to play the violin!" said Violet, starting to cry again.

"Of course you shall!" said Jessie. "I know Grandfather will buy you a violin, and Joe can teach you how to play it."

"It's not that," said Violet. "You see, I want to practice, and it's so *selfish* to go off and practice all by myself when I ought to be helping—"

Henry came in with the flashlight.

"Oh, my goodness!" cried Jessie. "What can I say? You talk to her, Henry!"

"I heard most of it," said Henry. "She thinks she's selfish to practice, when we came down here to have a good time together. Is that it?"

"That's just it," said Jessie.

"Now Violet, look here," said Henry. "You couldn't be selfish if you tried. We all want you to learn to play the violin. Most people don't even like to practice, you know."

Henry's little talk with Violet made her feel better. Soon they were all talking again, and even laughing a little.

"Sh!" said Jessie. "We'd better be quiet, we don't want to wake Benny. He would certainly howl."

The children left Violet feeling happy again, and thinking about the little violin her grandfather would surely buy for her.

The next morning, Joe got Captain Daniel to telephone Mr. Alden. He listened to the story, and thought about his own beautiful violin carefully packed away.

But he said to Captain Daniel, "Certainly, Violet must have a violin. The only trouble is that I am too busy this morning to buy one for her."

"Joe thinks he could pick one out," said Captain Daniel. "His playing is just wonderful."

"That Joe is a very interesting man," replied Mr. Alden. "I'll have a talk with him when I come over. Give him the money for the violin, Captain, and let him buy one if he thinks he can."

When Joe came back to the Alden Island with the little violin, Violet was waiting for him on the dock. Joe was sure that Violet could some day be a wonderful player, so he had bought her a fine violin.

The rest of the family came flying down to see if

Joe had had any luck. After they all had seen the violin, Violet shut the box.

"I don't think it likes to be outdoors," she said.

"I don't think so, either," agreed Joe. "Let's take it to the hut, and I will give you your first lesson."

"I'll go with you," said Benny.

"No, you had better stay on the dock with us and fish," said Henry quickly.

"Are you going to fish?" asked Benny.

"Yes!" said Henry, who had not thought of fishing until that very minute. "Just think, Benny, we've been here by the ocean four weeks and we haven't had a single fishing trip yet."

Suddenly Henry found that he wanted to go fishing himself.

"You will find fishlines and bait in an old box under the dock," called Joe.

Luck was surely with Henry. He baited a hook with a clam. Then he let down a long line and gave the end to Benny. Almost at once Benny began to yell and pull away on his line, hand over hand.

"Good!" cried Henry when Benny finally landed the fish on the dock. "What a wonderful fisherman you are, Benny! Wait, I'll take it off the hook for you, and put it on a string."

"What a big one!" said Jessie. "Don't catch many more of those, Benny, or we'll be eating fish for a week."

The children sat on the dock for a long time, but nothing happened.

"I wish I could catch one," said Jessie. "Another fish like the one Benny caught and we would have enough for dinner. And I know just how to bake them with dressing."

"I'm getting tired of this," said Henry. "I'm going to stop."

"I'm not," said Benny. "My grandfather told me fishing takes lots of time."

"He did take you fishing once, didn't he?" said Henry. "I remember I wanted to go, but I had to do school work."

"He told me that if I think I won't catch a fish, then I will catch one for sure. And so when I do catch one, I am surprised," said Benny.

"I see," said Henry, sitting down again. He tied his own line to the dock. And because he really did not think he would get any fish, he looked out at the boats. Henry had just sat down when Benny shouted, "Hurry! You've got a fish! Don't you see your line pull?"

Benny jumped for Henry's line and before anyone could help him, he pulled in another fish just like the first one.

"Oh, Jessie! Isn't that something? They are two twins, I guess!"

"I guess you are the fisherman of this family, all right," said Henry. "You and Grandfather. I don't even know when there is a fish on my own line."

Henry put a string through the mouth of the other fish, and Benny carried them proudly home.

"Joe can clean them for me," said Benny.

"Oh, I can do that!" said Henry. "I can clean fish, even if I can't catch them."

"Cut them in half, Henry, will you?" called Jessie. "I will go in and start the dressing."

Benny would not leave his twin fishes even for a minute. After Henry had washed them, Benny brought them to Jessie, and stayed by her side while she put them in a pan. Jessie piled the dressing made of bread, onions, melted butter, and salt on four pieces of fish.

"I guess they will be good," said Benny, as the oven door shut. He sat by the oven with the dog, until Jessie said that it was dinner time.

Violet came in. She put her violin carefully away, but she did not talk about her lesson.

"What do I smell?" she cried.

"It's the twins," said Benny. "They are in the oven baking."

"Twins!" cried Violet. "What does he mean?"

Jessie opened the oven door and took out the pan to show her.

"They are done. We can each have half a fish," she said. "And Benny shall have his first, because he caught them." She put the fish carefully on four plates.

"I wish Grandfather could see us eating your fish, Benny," said Henry. "You are a very good fisherman."

"He's coming to visit us tomorrow," said Violet. "He telephoned to Captain Daniel and said he would be over tomorrow, if it was all right."

"It's all right with me," cried Henry.

"And me," said Jessie. "But what shall we have to eat? I suppose we ought to have some meat for dinner."

"I think Grandfather would like to eat just what we do," said Violet.

"Maybe Grandfather and I could go fishing," said Benny, "but we might not catch anything."

"Grandfather won't have time to go fishing, Benny," said Henry. "Let's have dinner from our own garden. Remember those little vegetables we had in the boxcar days, Benny?"

"Oh, yes, little vegetables with melted butter!" cried Benny. "Let's have vegetables."

"That's a better idea. Then we'll be sure to have some dinner," said Jessie, laughing.

Chapter 10

Grandfather's Visit

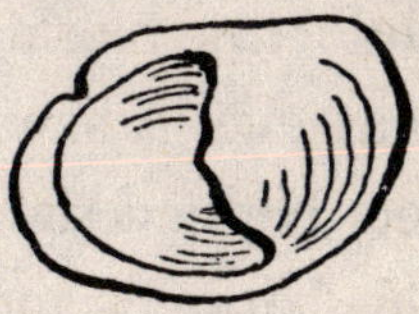

"We must be ready at ten o'clock," said Jessie the next morning. "Grandfather told Captain Daniel to meet him with the boat at ten o'clock and he is always on time."

"We must certainly show him the museum," said Henry. "I know he will be interested in the Indian things, but I'm not so sure about the birds and flowers."

"I think he will like our museum," said Violet. "It has his name on the door." She looked up and read the sign again, "THE JAMES H. ALDEN MUSEUM."

"Everything is ready," said Jessie. She took one last look. "Let's go down on the dock to wait for him."

Mr. Alden was delighted to see his grandchildren all waving from the dock.

"Fine children," he said to Captain Daniel.

"Best that ever I saw," agreed Captain Daniel, waving, too. He tied the boat and watched the old man and his happy grandchildren as they went out of sight into the barn.

"I want to see every single thing you have," said Mr. Alden. He sat down in the company chair and looked around him. "Say, what's this I see? A museum?"

Grandfather was on his feet in a minute. "Are you going to let me see it?" he asked excitedly, with his foot on the stairs.

"Of course!" cried Jessie. "If you don't mind the heat. It's awfully hot up there."

"No, I don't mind," said Mr. Alden at the top of

The James H. Alden Museum
Indian Exhibit

the stairs. He saw what the museum was like, with one look. "Which one of you thought of this? Tell me about it."

They told him all about their museum. They showed him the flowers, the seaweed, the boxes of shells and butterflies, and the paper birds in real branches.

Mr. Alden looked for a long time at the bluebird sitting near its nest. There were four blue eggs cut from paper in the nest.

"The birds left that nest," said Henry, "so we took it."

"Good!" said Mr. Alden, smiling. "And what did you find, Benny?"

"I found a big bone in the shell-pile."

"We ought to tell you about that bone, Grandfather," said Henry, laughing. "Let's go downstairs and you can sit in the company chair. You see we found the skeleton of a whole Indian, and Benny found his leg bone. Joe says it is very important and not to tell anyone but you."

"Where is this skeleton?" cried Mr. Alden.

"It's near a very big pile of shells on the end of the island."

"Yes, I remember seeing that pile of shells when I was a boy," said Mr. Alden.

"Joe told us not to pick up the Indian bones," said Benny. "He said you could get men to do it right after we go home."

"That Joe seems to know a lot," said Mr. Alden. "I'll see him before I go."

"Look in this box, Grandfather," said Benny. "That's an arrowhead, and that's an ax-head, and that's a cooking bowl, all Indian. And that's a tool made out of bone. Watch found the ax-head and the tool."

"Well, well!" cried Mr. Alden. "Who told you? Did anyone tell you to make a museum to put these things in?"

"No," said Henry. "Don't you *like* it?"

"Yes, Henry, I like it very much indeed. It just seems strange, because it's the very thing I used to do myself. I used to go out in the woods all alone and sit for hours listening to the birds."

"Yes," said Henry, smiling. "We do the very same thing; we must be just like you."

Then Violet brought her violin for him to see. To their surprise, Mr. Alden put it under his chin and began to play. He played very well.

"You didn't know I played, did you?" said Mr. Alden to the surprised children. "That's a fine little violin, Violet."

"You're a wonderful grandfather!" cried Henry. "Always doing something new! We didn't know you could play."

"I am out of practice," said Mr. Alden, handing the violin back to Violet. "Haven't even held a violin for years. Now what else have you to show me?"

"You must come to the little hut to see Joe," said Benny.

"I think Joe went over to the mainland this morning," said Violet.

"That's funny," said Henry, "because he certainly knew you were coming today."

"It makes me cross," shouted Benny. "I want you to see Joe. He's my best friend in all the world."

"Then I'm cross, too," said Mr. Alden. "What time do you have dinner around here?"

"Almost right away!" cried Jessie. "Are you hungry?"

"I am hungry as a bear," answered Mr. Alden.

At once, Jessie put some water in the big kettle. "You children set the table and get the milk out, so that Grandfather won't have to wait a minute after dinner is ready."

"Oh, you needn't hurry as much as that," said Mr. Alden. "I can wait half an hour, maybe."

Before that time, the little vegetables were done. Jessie put them in a big dish and poured melted butter over them. There was plenty of bread and butter to go along with the vegetables. And because they had company, Jessie had put two eggs and some sugar into the milk.

"This is a delicious drink!" said Mr. Alden. "I shall come again."

"Please do!" cried Violet. "But you're not going home for a long time yet, I hope?"

"I think I am," said Mr. Alden, "and I should like

to take you all with me. Just on a little trip for an hour or so," he added quickly.

"All right," said Jessie. "I thought for a minute that you wanted us to leave the island for good."

"You like it, don't you? No, it won't take very long. I want to show you something."

It did not take long for Captain Daniel to get the family to the mainland. They got into Mr. Alden's waiting car and were taken to a big building they had never seen before.

"It's a museum!" cried Henry. "Look, Jessie, *look!*"

Henry pointed at the name over the door, which said in large letters cut in stone, THE ALDEN MUSEUM.

"My goodness!" cried Jessie. "Is that named for you, Grandfather?"

"I suppose it is," said Mr. Alden. "It has been here a long time."

"You gave the money to build it!" cried Henry.

The surprised children followed their grandfather inside, where a young girl came and showed them everything he wanted them to see. At last they came to a small room, and the girl told them to go in. Jessie was the first to see a sign which read, THE FIRST COLLECTION MADE BY JAMES HENRY ALDEN WHEN HE WAS A BOY OF FIFTEEN.

"What do you know!" cried Henry, looking at the birds. "Our birds are just like yours!"

Mr. Alden's birds were painted ones, too, and they were sitting in real trees.

"The birds left these nests," said Mr. Alden with a twinkle in his eyes, "so I took them."

Henry laughed and said, "You didn't want to kill any birds either, did you?"

Mr. Alden went on, "No, the real birds out in the museum were found dead and brought to us. Not a bird in this museum was killed for me. And now, I'll let you go back to your island and wash your dishes."

When they got into the boat, he gave them each a box. And it was not until later that he remembered that he had not seen Joe, the handy man.

Chapter 11

Apple Pie

The next morning was very cold. Benny did not want to get up at all.

"No," he said, "it is so cold that I'm not going to get out of bed."

Henry looked out at the ocean. "I have an idea," he said. "It's too cold outside today. Let's all stay inside and paint our birds."

"Fine!" agreed Jessie. "I'll light the stove and we'll shut the barn door. It will soon be warm."

In spite of what he had said earlier about staying in bed, Benny opened the swinging door of his room, and came out wearing his red sweater. He was carrying the little toy boat which was in the package his grandfather had given him.

"I like my new boat," said Benny, proudly. "Let's make it go, Henry."

"Put it in that pail of water, Benny," said Henry. "You play with your boat while we get ready to work."

The girls helped Henry put the table in the corner under the window. Then Jessie brought the bird books and some heavy paper.

"I'm going to use my new pen," said Violet. "Grandfather knew I needed a new one."

"He knew I wanted a set of things like this, to fix cuts," said Henry. "It will be handy to have when we go on picnics or exploring."

Grandfather had given Jessie a set of six cooking spoons.

"Are you going to use your new spoons today, Jessie?" asked Violet.

"I might," said Jessie. "I have a good idea for dinner this noon. I think you'll like it, but I won't tell you what it is until we have finished painting the birds."

"Let's get to work, then!" cried Henry. "I'll cut out paper birds and you girls color them."

"Cut out a picture of every bird we have seen," said Jessie. "The bird book tells all the names."

The children worked all morning. Suddenly Benny said, "Henry, I think Joe ought to have stayed here to see Grandfather."

"I think so, too," said Henry.

"It seems very strange," said Violet, "for him to go off without telling us."

"We'll ask him when he comes back," said Jessie. "And now, I'll tell you my surprise for dinner. I am going to make an apple pie."

"But you never made a pie," said Henry, looking up.

"No," said Jessie, "but I'm going to now."

She took a pan of very small green apples out of the cupboard.

"Where did you get them?" asked Benny.

"Near the yellow house," said Jessie. "There are two apple trees there."

"I'll get them ready," said Violet.

"Good! And Henry, won't you smooth off one of those boards for a pie-board?"

Jessie washed the new board. Then she picked up a big empty green bottle. "This is my rolling pin," she said. "I am going to try to make some good pie crust."

So over and over she rolled the crust. She put some butter on it and rolled it out again. But when Jessie put the bottom crust in the pan, the crust was not big enough.

"Put a patch in it," said Benny.

Jessie took a little more crust and smoothed it over the edge of the pan with her fingers. "This

is going to be a very deep pie," she said. "And there will be lots of apples in it."

Benny watched Jessie roll out the top crust. "Make it big enough this time, Jessie," he said. "There are lots of apples."

Jessie rolled the top crust a little thinner. It was just right. When the pie was in the oven, she began to boil some sugar and water in a saucepan.

"What's that for?" asked Henry. He began to take the things off the table.

"Just wait," said Jessie. "I think it's going to be the best thing about this pie. You see there isn't any sugar in the pie yet, so there is no juice to boil over. Why don't you get out the bread and milk and set the table? Then everything else will be ready when the pie is done."

When the crust was nice and brown, Jessie took the pie out of the oven. She lifted up the top crust with a knife, and carefully poured the hot juice over the apples. Then she let down the crust again.

Just as Jessie was about to cut the pie into four pieces, there was a knock at the barn door.

"Who in the world can that be?" cried Henry. He was so surprised that he almost dropped his cup.

When Henry opened the door, he was even more surprised to see a tall man standing there.

"I'm sorry," said the stranger, "but I went to the fisherman's hut, and nobody was at home."

"Won't you come in?" asked Jessie.

"Thank you. It is a cold day," said the man with a smile. "Oh, I see that you are about to have dinner. I'll just stay long enough to ask you something."

"Won't you sit down?" said Henry.

"Thank you. My name is Browning," he said as he sat down in the company chair. "A young man who went exploring for me last year has been lost. I heard that he was dead. Then later I heard that he was living on the Alden Island. This is the Alden Island, isn't it?"

"Yes," said Henry. "But there is nobody on the island but Captain Daniel and his friend Joe."

"Who is this Captain Daniel?" asked Mr. Browning.

"Oh, Captain Daniel is old," said Henry, "and

I'm sure he never went exploring. He has been with my grandfather for years."

"How about his friend Joe?" asked the man.

"He's nice. He's my best friend in all the world," said Benny, proudly "all but Jessie, and maybe Watch and Captain Daniel—and of course Violet and Henry and my grandfather —"

"You have a lot of best friends," said the man, laughing. "Tell me, what color are Joe's eyes and hair?"

"He has brown hair and brown eyes," said Benny, "and he has a violin."

"I don't think he is the one I know, then," said the man. "I never heard that he played the violin. Just the same, I should like to see your Joe."

"Won't you wait for him? He is sure to come back soon," said Jessie. "Why don't you stay to dinner and help us eat our first apple pie?"

The man looked at the big pie and said, "If you are sure there will be enough, I think I will."

So the pie was cut into five pieces. Violet quietly

got an extra cup of milk and set another place, and the stranger sat down to a strange dinner.

"When I look at that pie," said Mr. Browning, "my mouth fills up with water." And certainly everyone was watching Jessie as she took out the big juicy pieces.

"Milk seems to go with apple pie," said Henry.

"I never knew pie could be so delicious," said Mr. Browning when dinner was over. "But now, if I may, I think I will see if I can find Joe."

"We think that Joe is more than a handy man," said Henry.

"Joe knows everything in the world," said Benny. "He knows all the flowers and the birds and the clam shells, and Indian things."

"Indian things!" cried Mr. Browning. "It must be the very one. He was the head of a museum before he went away. I *must* see him."

But Mr. Browning did not see Joe. Captain Daniel came back to the island without him. He said that Joe had gone away for a day or two.

"Is he coming back?" asked Benny, getting ready to howl.

"Oh, yes," said Captain Daniel. "He will come back, all right."

When Mr. Browning left, he told Jessie that he was glad he came, for now he had met a girl who could make a wonderful apple pie with an old green bottle for a rolling pin.

Chapter 12

The Picnic

The children were waiting upon the dock when Joe came back. But it was too late then to find Mr. Browning.

Jessie began, "You know, Joe, Grandfather said we should never build a fire outdoors unless someone older helped us. Now we have such a good place for a picnic, we thought we'd invite our school friends over for a picnic on the beach. They have never seen the island."

"I'll be glad to help you build a fire, if that's what you want," said Joe.

"Oh, thanks, Joe," said Jessie.

The four children invited their friends over Captain Daniel's telephone. All of them said that they would come. Henry's friend was a tall boy named Morris Wilder, and Jessie's friend was Morris' sister, Marjorie. Violet invited her friend, Barbara Black. Benny surprised them by saying that he wanted to invite Mike Wood, a little boy who was always in trouble.

"Mike and Benny will be quite a pair!" cried Henry. "But I suppose he can invite anyone he likes. We all did."

"We'll have fish chowder for dinner," said Jessie. "We can always get some fish from Captain Daniel."

"And we'll all pick blueberries after the others get here," said Henry. "That will be something to do."

When the guests arrived, Watch was very excited. Mike had brought his big white dog, Spotty, with him. Jessie had a hard time trying to keep the dogs from fighting, but after a lot of barking Watch and Spotty were friends.

"Let's race the dogs, Ben," cried Mike, who could never be still very long.

The two boys held the dogs for a minute, and then let them go. Both dogs seemed to understand, for they raced to the beach where they dropped, panting, on the sand beside Joe. Watch knew the way, and got there first.

"Spotty got there first!" shouted Mike.

"He did not!" cried Benny. "He didn't even know the way!"

"Benny, Benny!" said Henry. "Don't start the picnic fighting."

"Watch got there first and you know it," said Benny.

"Spotty is better than Watch," said Mike.

"Spotty is not better than Watch!" shouted Benny. "Watch can run faster than Spotty, and he got there first in the race!"

"You started this fight, Ben!" said Mike.

"I did not start it!" shouted Benny.

"Yes, you did, too!" shouted Mike.

"Now, you listen to me, young fellow," said Morris, catching Mike's hand. "You stop, or you'll have to go home."

Mike began to jump up and down, when suddenly he jumped on a very sharp shell. Then Mike sat down holding his foot and crying at the same time. Henry sat down, too, and tried to look at Mike's foot. He took out his box of things for fixing cuts.

"Keep still, now, Mike," he said. "You've got a long cut here, but it's not deep. Let me fix it."

The cut foot was a big help to everyone. It kept

Mike in sight all morning, while the four older children and Joe picked blueberries.

At noon, Jessie and Violet watched while Joe made a fire and boiled some water. Henry and Morris cut the potatoes and onions and the chowder was soon ready.

Everyone enjoyed the chowder, and the boys had made enough extra for supper, too. After blueberries and milk, Jessie and Violet washed the dishes in the ocean, while Benny and Mike walked away slowly.

"Keep an eye on Mike, Henry," said Jessie.

"I can see them. They are just sitting over there on the rocks," said Henry.

But the next time he looked, the boys had gone.

"Where could they go?" he cried, getting up quickly. "There's no place for them to go, because I can see the whole beach!"

But the little boys were not in sight. As Henry climbed upon the rocks, he was very glad to hear Benny's voice.

"I wonder who left the bottle here?" said Benny.

Henry and Morris looked under the rocks into a tiny cave.

"How in the world did you boys get in there?" asked Henry.

"The stone came off," said Benny. "It was like a door, and we pulled it away. It was awfully heavy."

"Say, you fellows climb out of there and let us go in," said Morris. The little boys obeyed at once and the two older boys crawled in and looked around. They saw a big stone table with an old bottle on it.

"Let's take out the bottle," said Henry. "There may be something inside."

"Look, Joe," said Morris. "See what Ben and Mike found."

"There's a paper inside the bottle," said Henry. "Shall we take it out?"

"Why not?" said Joe, turning it over. "Maybe there's a name on the paper."

"Let me get the paper out with my knife," said Henry. The mouth of the bottle was just wide enough for the knife. Henry pulled the paper out easily and read, " 'If found, give to J. Alden. Six feet from cross to red rock, and three feet down. J. A. and R. W.' "

"Grandfather must have left it here when he was a boy," said Henry, "but I don't see any cross."

"I do," said Mike. "It's right over there." He pointed at a strange rock. It did look like a cross.

"And there's the red rock!" cried Violet. "See!"

"This will be easy," said Morris. "You run a string from the cross straight to the red rock. Then what does it say?" He looked at the paper again. "Six feet. Well, six feet from the cross you dig down for three feet. There must be something *there*."

The children were excited as they tied the string to the red rock. Joe showed them where six feet would be. Then they took turns digging with a spoon. With Watch and Spotty to help, they dug a hole three feet deep, but there was nothing in it but water. After an hour's digging they had still not found anything.

"We can dig some other day," said Henry at last. "It may be down twelve feet since the paper is very old."

All the children but Mike were tired and were glad to sit down on the grass. The little fellow still sat beside the hole with Spotty, digging away with the spoon. Then suddenly he began to shout.

"It's mine, all mine, because I found it. You can't say it isn't, because you all stopped digging."

When the children ran to the hole, they saw Mike pulling out a black box covered with wet sand. And Mike went right on shouting.

"I found the cave, too, and made Ben help me take the door off, and I found the cross and I dug out the box, and it's mine!"

"Don't talk so much. Of course it's yours, Mike," said Henry. "Why don't you open it?"

It was not hard to do this, because the box was very old. Mike pulled off the cover with his fingers, and the children saw a pile of old money. Mike put the money, one piece at a time, in the cover of the box.

"Just five dollars!" said Morris. "What a lot of money, Mike!"

"Grandfather will give him a five-dollar bill," said Jessie. "I think he would like to keep this old money he put here when he was a boy. Wouldn't you like to have a new five-dollar bill, Mike?"

"Y-yes, of course," said Mike who had never had even a dollar bill before in his whole life.

Just then, the children heard a shout coming over the water. Then they noticed a boy in a rowboat who was standing up, shouting, and pointing at the water.

A dark head showed for a minute and then went out of sight.

"There's somebody in the water, too!" cried Morris.

Henry heard Joe say to himself, "I'm well, now. I'm not afraid."

Joe took off his shoes, jumped into the water, and swam very fast. "Bring the boat here!" he shouted to the boy in the boat.

But the boat went right past him.

"Oh, come back, Joe!" cried Benny.

"He'll come back, all right," said Morris. "He's a wonderful swimmer! Look!"

As Morris spoke, Joe swam under water suddenly. When he came up he was pulling the boy to the rowboat. It seemed hours before Joe finally got the boy into the boat and pulled himself in.

"Good for Joe!" shouted Henry. "I hope he got there in time."

"Everybody ought to know how to swim," said Morris. "That boy was afraid. He just stood there and yelled. He couldn't even bring the boat over when Joe asked him to."

All this time Mike had not said anything. He stood very still as he looked out over the water. The little fellow seemed to have turned to stone.

"Why are you so scared?" asked Henry.

"I think it's Pat," said Mike, still staring at the boat.

"Pat? Who is he?" asked Henry.

"He's my brother," said Mike. "He's eleven years old. I think he was the one in the water."

"You can't see that far," said Morris. "What makes you think so, Mike?"

"Well, I told him there would be something to eat at this picnic, and that maybe we'd play ball."

"I begin to see," said Henry, looking at Morris. "Do you know who the other boy is?"

"Maybe Johnny," said Mike. "I told Johnny, too, and he knew about a rowboat he could get."

"How did they get the boat?" asked Morris.

"They just *took* it," said Mike.

"What an awful thing to do!" shouted Henry. "Besides, they can't swim or row."

It did seem so, for Joe was rowing. One boy was out of sight in the boat, and the other boy sat at one end. When Jessie saw the boat coming, she called to Marjorie, "Let's run to the barn and get some blankets and towels."

"Good for you, Jessie!" called Joe when the girls brought the blankets. "Lay them down on the other side of the fire."

Jessie and Marjorie spread out the blankets, while Henry and Morris caught the boat as it landed on the beach.

"It is Pat," said Mike in a frightened voice. "Isn't it, Johnny?"

"Yes," said Johnny. "But he'll be all right. This man said so."

"He's lucky," said Henry. "Lucky that Joe knew how to swim."

Pat was very still when the boys helped Joe lift him out of the boat and roll him in a blanket by the fire.

"We won't talk to him now," said Joe, rubbing the boy's hair with a towel. "We'll let him sleep first. He's all tired out."

"I guess you won't have to talk to him," said Johnny, who was very white. "We won't ever take a boat again."

"No, I don't believe you will, either," called Joe, as he went back to the hut for dry clothes.

Just then, Mike said, "Pat didn't get any dinner. Will you heat up the chowder for him, Henry?"

"He can't eat when he's sound asleep, can he?" asked Morris.

"No, but he'll wake up when he smells the chowder," said Mike. "Maybe I could have some more myself, because I didn't eat much lunch."

"Ho, I should say you didn't!" said Morris. "Only three bowls full!"

"I'll tell you what we can do," said Joe, who had come back wearing dry clothes. "We have just enough to play ball, if Mike is eating and doesn't want to play."

"Oh, I want to play! I want to play!" shouted Mike, jumping up and forgetting about the cut on his foot.

And so all the children played ball. Later, there was more chowder for everyone, and Pat did wake up when he smelled the food.

"This is the best picnic I've ever been to," said Mike, passing his bowl again.

"Hold on, there!" warned Joe. "Don't give him any more, Henry. Six bowls of chowder in one day are enough for one small boy."

Just then Captain Daniel came with the boat to take the children home. And now Benny began to cry because his friend was going.

"Ho! What are you crying about, Ben?" asked Mike. "I wouldn't cry at nothing."

So nobody cried when the company started for home in the boat. When Mike could not hear

Benny's answer, he put his two hands up to his mouth and shouted, "Spotty can run—faster—than —Watch!"

"Well, Benny, don't you care," said Henry. "Just be glad the day is over with no more trouble."

"You're right," said Joe. "What a day!"

Then Henry remembered that Joe had said he was well again. And when Henry told Jessie about it later, she thought it was very strange, too.

Chapter 13

Joe Again

I wish Mike would come over every day," said Benny one morning.

"Well, I don't!" said all the others at once.

Henry looked up. "I think we can get along without any company at all."

"You don't call Joe company, do you?" asked Violet.

"Oh, no," said Henry. "He's just one of the family. Why? Did you want to invite him to eat with us?"

"No," said Violet slowly. "But today he said I would be ready to play to you after my lesson."

"Have him stay to supper," said Jessie. She looked at Henry.

"Benny, come here," said Henry. "Did you know that today is your birthday?"

"No," said Benny, walking over to his brother.

"Well, it is," Henry went on, "and now what do you want for a present? We will buy it for you."

"Cream," said Benny.

"Do you mean ice-cream?" asked Henry.

"No, I don't. I mean cream in a bottle like milk. A big bottle . . . not a little one."

"That's a queer kind of a present," said Violet.

"You want to drink it?" asked Jessie.

"No, I want to put it on some blackberries, like Peter Rabbit."

"We'll get a big bottle of cream then, Jessie," said Henry, laughing.

Benny began to jump around the barn and yell.

"Benny," said Jessie, "Violet is going to bake you a birthday cake before she takes her lesson."

"Is she?" asked Benny, giving a last yell. "I want to watch her make my cake."

Violet got out her cooking things. She laid everything she needed on the pie-board.

"We will put the candles around the cake," said Violet.

"I want a candle in the middle," said Benny.

"Yes, but we want to save the middle—" Violet stopped suddenly.

"Never mind," said Jessie. "Benny doesn't know what we want to save the middle for."

The cake looked wonderful. And when Violet

took it out of the oven, Benny said, "It smells just like a birthday cake."

Before she put the frosting on, Violet put the cake on two plates to get cold.

"Let's sit down," said Jessie, "and have a quick lunch of bread and milk. Then Henry can get the cream and candles, and Violet can take her lesson while I wash the dishes."

"I'll wipe the dishes for you," said Benny.

"Aren't you a good boy!" cried Jessie. "And on your birthday, too. You will have a happy birthday, I'm sure."

They were just finishing when Joe and Violet came in carrying their violins.

"Violet is ready to play for you," said Joe. "Will everyone please sit down?"

Jessie was excited as she sat down on one of the boxes between Henry and Benny. Violet did not seem to be either excited or afraid. It was the first time she had played for anyone besides Joe. She waited now, holding her violin, for her teacher to tell her where to stand.

Joe told Violet to stand facing the door. He stood with his back to the wall, where he could watch Violet. Then they began to play. Violet's part was very easy, but Joe's part was hard. It seemed to be only Violet's playing that the children heard. Violet did not seem like their sister.

"Beautiful!" cried Jessie at the end.

"She's good, isn't she?" asked Joe, turning around.

"Wonderful!" said Henry. "She could be a real violin player, couldn't she, Joe?"

"She could be, and she *will* be," replied Joe.

"I wish Violet would play it again, so I would get used to it," said Benny.

"Do play it again," said Jessie. "I could listen all day."

Violet and Joe began to play the piece again. When they were halfway through it, Mr. Browning appeared at the barn door. Violet looked up and smiled, but she did not stop playing.

When the piece was finished, Mr. Browning cried, "John!"

Joe turned around and said, "Oh, Mr. Browning!"

He held out his hand. "I'm really glad to see you. Everything is all right again."

"Well, I'm glad to see *you*, my boy!" said Mr. Browning. "I have been looking for you for a long time."

"Here are my friends," said Joe. "This is Jessie —"

"Oh, we did meet Mr. Browning," said Jessie, with a smile. "We know him quite well. Please everybody sit down."

"I could never forget the girl who makes apple pies with a green bottle," said Mr. Browning, taking the company chair. "Or this little girl who plays the violin so well. You see, children, this Joe of yours is my best friend."

"He's my best friend," said Benny.

"Yes, I think you told me so, when I was here before," answered the man, looking at Benny. "But he was my best friend before he was yours."

Benny thought this over, "He could have two best friends," he said.

"Good for you! Will you let me ask him where he has been, and what is the matter with him?"

"Nothing is the matter with Joe," said Benny.

"That's right," said Joe. "I wasn't well for a long time and for a while I didn't even remember who I was. I'll tell you all about it later. Now, I'm better, and ready to go back to the museum. And to my uncle, if he'll have me."

"Have you!" said Mr. Browning. "Your uncle has almost worn himself out worrying about you."

"Then the sooner, the better," said Joe.

"He works in a museum," thought Henry.

"He is a very clever man," thought Jessie.

"Did you really think Joe was a handy man working for Captain Daniel?" asked Mr. Browning.

"N-no," said Henry. "I thought he worked in a museum, but was taking some time off."

"I began wondering when he got us all those books," said Violet. "He found the names of the shells and flowers right away."

"Joe," said Jessie, "did you write all those books? I remember we said the name on the books is just like ours."

Joe smiled, but he didn't say anything.

"I don't think you know yet who he is!" cried Mr. Browning.

"I do," said Benny. "He knows more than what is in all those books, and he works in a museum."

"That's right," said Mr. Browning. "He is the head of a museum. Do you think his name is Joseph Alden?"

"Yes," said Benny. "I think that, too."

"Well, it is. It is John Joseph Alden," said Mr. Browning. "But you don't understand yet. He is your cousin."

"What!" cried the children together.

"Yes," said Mr. Browning. "Joe's father and your grandfather were brothers."

"Joe, did you ever *live* with Grandfather?" asked Henry.

Joe looked at his cousins and said, "I used to live there before I went away, and now I think I'll go back. That is, if Uncle James will have me and my cousins don't mind?"

"Mind!" cried Henry. "It would be wonderful!"

"Oh, Joe!" shouted Benny. "You can keep on knowing things all the time. I'd rather have you live with us than even Watch!"

And nobody could say more than that.

Chapter 14

Everybody's Birthday

"Somebody had better call Grandfather right away," said Henry.

"Let me," said Benny. "It's my birthday."

Later, when Benny came back from Captain Daniel's hut, he said, "Grandfather is coming today, and he's bringing Dr. Moore and his mother."

"That's great," said Henry. "We'll have a big party."

Then Benny said to Joe, "Are you going to tell Grandfather that he's your grandfather, too?"

"He isn't my grandfather, Benny. He's my uncle."

"All right, are you going to tell him that he's your uncle?" asked Benny.

"He will know me as soon as he sees me," replied Joe.

Mr. Browning said, "I don't think he had better see you suddenly, John. He must be very sad because he thinks he has lost you. Sudden news like this is not good for an old man."

"Let Jessie fix it," said Joe. "I will stay in the hut until you tell me it's all right."

Jessie promised to do her best.

Joe went back to Captain Daniel's hut to wait. In a few minutes they could see the motorboat coming, and soon Mr. Alden and the Moores were on the dock.

"Hello, Grandfather!" cried Benny. "It's my birthday!"

"Well, so it is!" replied Mr. Alden. "Happy birthday, my boy!"

Then everyone began to speak at once.

"That's a big basket you have," said Jessie to Dr. Moore.

"Sh, sh!" said the doctor, laughing. He took out another big basket just like it and some packages. "Presents," he whispered to Jessie.

"I got a big bottle of cream for my birthday, Grandfather," said Benny.

"It was funny, Grandfather," said Jessie, half laughing. "That's all he wanted, so we got it."

"You did right, my dear," said Mr. Alden. "People should have what they want on birthdays."

"I got lots of surprises today," Benny went on.

"He doesn't know them all himself, yet," said Jessie quickly. She didn't know what Benny might say next.

"This island is just full of surprises, and that would be a good name for it—Surprise Island."

"It would!" cried Henry. "Just think of all the surprises we've had. Let's call it Surprise Island."

"I think that's a wonderful name," said Mrs. Moore. "I hope they were all good surprises."

"Every one," said Henry, trying to get Benny to think of something else. "There were clams, and the Indian things, and the violin."

"And my birthday," said Benny. "Are your veins all right, Grandfather?"

"Veins?" asked Mr. Alden.

"Yes," said Benny. "You know some people have funny veins, so when they hear something awfully good, *suddenly*, they just drop down dead."

"I am sure that good news wouldn't kill me," said Mr. Alden. "Now, Mrs. Moore, just look at that white sand! Isn't it beautiful?"

"It certainly is," said Mrs. Moore.

"It's very good sand for houses, too," said Benny, running down to it.

"Let's build a house, then," said Dr. Moore, putting down the baskets.

Jessie was trying to think of exactly the right way to tell her grandfather about Joe. She had not wanted to tell the news too suddenly, but Benny seemed to have made it easy.

"I suppose Benny is right about the veins, isn't he, Grandfather?" she said.

"I suppose so," said Mr. Alden, laughing. He sat down on a rock. "But I never could understand it.

If I had good news, I wouldn't want to miss the fun."

"That sounds right to me," said Henry, laughing.

Jessie could not wait any longer. "We have a wonderful surprise for you, Grandfather!" she said, getting up. "Come! You know what you promised about the veins?"

"You can't drop dead, because you promised!" shouted Benny.

"What do you mean?" asked Mr. Alden, looking very white. He started to go with the excited children.

"Think of the nicest surprise you can," said Henry. "What would that thing be?"

"It wouldn't be a *thing;* it would be a man," said Mr. Alden.

"That's all right!" cried Jessie. "It is a man!"

Violet took her grandfather's hand. "Are you too worn out to run just a little way, now? Joe is so worried."

"Joe?" said Mr. Alden. But then he saw two men coming along.

"My dear John!" cried Mr. Alden. Joe ran up and took his uncle's hands.

"Uncle James, I want you to meet my good friend, Mr. Browning," said Joe.

"I am glad to meet you, Mr. Browning," said Mr. Alden as they shook hands.

Then he turned to Joe. "But why didn't you come home, John? Why didn't you come right to me?"

"Before I came home, I wanted to be sure I was all right," said Joe. "But first I went to old Captain Daniel on the island. I met Dr. Moore early this summer when he came with the children."

"Dr. Moore, do you mean you knew who he was all this time?" asked Mr. Alden.

"Yes," replied the doctor, "but I promised not to tell. I wanted to be sure myself that Joe was well again. Besides, it was a good way for him to get to know his new cousins."

"I got two presents for my birthday," said Benny, "a new cousin and a bottle of cream."

"I feel as if it were my birthday," said Joe, looking at him.

"And so do I," agreed Mr. Alden.

"I think it's my birthday, too," said Mr. Browning, looking at his old friend.

"It's everybody's birthday," cried Jessie. "Can't you all come to the barn for our birthday supper? We can cut the cake into tiny slices."

"I thought of that, also, Jessie," said Mrs. Moore, going over to the little housekeeper. "I brought over some sliced ham and other food in those two big baskets. I hope you don't mind? I hear you have blackberries and cream."

"And my birthday cake," said Benny.

"Oh, dear! I haven't put on the candles, yet! I haven't even frosted it!" cried Violet.

"Benny, you stay here with the men," said Jessie. "Mrs. Moore will help Henry and me while Violet frosts the cake."

Violet put some sugar and egg whites into a bowl. After the frosting was made, she put it on the cake, sides and all.

"Let's put the candles around the edge of the cake and 'Watch' in the middle," she said. One day Henry had bought a little toy dog that looked like Watch. The cake looked delicious when Violet put it into the little cupboard.

Mrs. Moore began to take things out of the baskets. Besides a large plate piled high with ham there were many other delicious things to eat.

Jessie was delighted that Mrs. Moore had brought some extra plates and a tablecloth. She helped Mrs. Moore put the white cloth carefully on the table. Violet set the birthday cake at Benny's place. Then she filled a bowl with purple and white flowers to put in the middle of the table.

When Benny saw the cake and the toy dog he laughed and said, "Ho, that looks just like Watch in the middle of my cake!"

Now everybody began to sit down around the table. Some sat on boxes, Grandfather sat on the company chair, and Joe sat on a block of wood.

Mrs. Moore passed the plate of ham to Benny.

"No, thank you," said Benny. "I don't want any ham. I just want blackberries and sugar and cream."

"Since it's his birthday party, let him have what he wants," said Jessie.

"I'll feel bad if you don't eat some cake," said Violet.

"All right," said Benny, "but after I eat my cake, I don't want anything except blackberries and cream, like Peter Rabbit."

"Only Peter Rabbit didn't get any. Don't you remember?" said Grandfather.

"He will this time," said Joe. "At last Peter Rabbit has his blackberries and cream, on his birthday."

"Everybody is happy, then," said Mr. Alden, looking around at the smiling faces. "And that is just right, because it is everybody's birthday."

Chapter 15

Good-by Summer

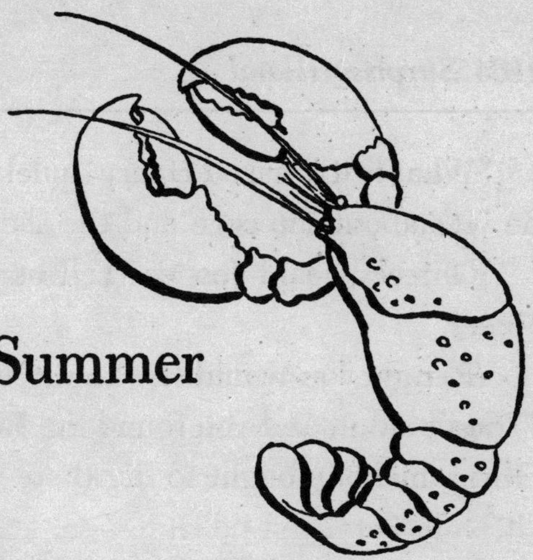

It was late summer and the children were sitting with Joe on the beach.

"We have to go home tonight," said Jessie sadly.

"Grandfather says he wants to take us on a trip before school begins," said Henry.

"I don't mind going home," said Violet. "I miss Grandfather, and he must have been lonesome, even if he didn't say so."

"I hope we can come again next summer," said Henry. "We have had such a good time."

"I'm glad we can sit down and talk quietly," said Joe, "because I want to tell you something. I hope you won't feel too bad about it."

"What is it?" asked Henry quickly.

"It's about the cave and the shell-pile," said Joe.

"Oh, yes," said Jessie. "Tell us the whole story, Joe."

"I know you would like to dig in that cave now. You found it, and you found the Indian things in it. But somebody ought to dig there who understands it."

"Meaning yourself?" asked Henry.

"No, not alone," replied Joe. "Your grandfather, my Uncle James, is letting a lot of men come to work at the cave. They are coming over with all their tools to dig very carefully so that they won't miss anything."

"That's all right," said Benny. "Couldn't we watch them?"

"Sometimes you could," said Joe. "Sometimes you couldn't. You see they are going to blow the top off the cave."

He watched the children as he said this.

"Oh, boy!" cried Benny. "That's the day I'd like to come."

"You would!" said Joe. "That's just the day you can't come."

Benny suddenly began yelling at the top of his voice, "I want to come the day they blow the top off the cave!"

And then he began to howl. Throwing himself down on the sand, he howled and yelled just as loudly as he could.

"My!" cried Joe, who had not heard Benny howl before. "Can't you stop him? Does he do that often?"

"No, not often," shouted Jessie over the noise.

"Listen, Benny," said Violet. "Stop crying and I'll build you a sand house."

But Benny still howled.

"Look here, Benny!" said Henry finally. "What will Joe think?"

In spite of anything they could say, Benny yelled on and on.

"I'm sorry," Henry said to Joe at last. "He will stop some time. Some day he'll grow up."

Just then a voice said very softly, "Please—" It was Captain Daniel.

"I came over," he began, but stopped because of the noise.

Benny opened one eye.

Captain Daniel went on a little louder, "I came over to see if you'd like to go with me when I get my lobsters."

At this, Benny opened the other eye and stopped howling. "I would," he said.

"Whew!" said Joe. "What a noise that was!"

"It was for sure," said Captain Daniel. "I heard it down in my boat."

"He hasn't howled all summer until today," said Henry. "He's getting over it."

"I hope so," said Joe.

"We'd like to go with you very much, Captain Daniel," said Jessie.

"Any time," said the captain.

"Let's go right now," said Benny, just as if he had never cried at all.

"All right, Captain, we're ready to go," said Henry.

Then everyone jumped up and climbed over the rocks with Captain Daniel to the motorboat.

As they scrambled into the boat, Benny asked, "Is it fun to get lobsters, Captain Daniel?"

"I enjoy it," answered the captain. "Your grandfather enjoys it, too. I promised him to take you out once before you went home."

There was a pail of fish-heads for bait in the bottom of the boat and a big empty box. Captain Daniel told them all where to sit.

"Sorry," said Captain Daniel, looking at Watch, "I don't think we'd better take the dog along. Can't you leave him?"

"I am not going either," said Joe. "I have to telephone a lot of people. Don't you think Watch would stay with me?"

"He will if Jessie tells him," said Henry.

"Listen, Watch," said Jessie. "Sit down here. Stay with Joe."

Watch obeyed and sat down.

"Good dog," said Jessie. "He understands."

Soon Captain Daniel started the motor, and the children waved good-by to Joe.

"How nice this is!" cried Jessie. She put her fingers in the water.

"I wish you had asked us to go with you before," said Henry. "It's wonderful!"

"Why is that red board floating out there?" asked Benny, pointing.

"Good boy!" cried Captain Daniel, very pleased. "That's one of my lobster floats. It shows the place where I have a lobster pot in the water. Good sharp eyes you have, Benny, to notice that."

As they came near the red board, Captain Daniel stopped the motor.

"Can you reach it, Henry?" he asked, as the boat stopped.

Henry caught the red float and began to lift it out of the water. A lot of rope came up, and at last a heavy lobster pot.

"Oh, you caught some lobsters!" shouted Benny. "Aren't they queer? These are different from real lobsters—they're green."

"All lobsters are green, Benny," said Jessie. "They turn red when they are cooked."

"Will these turn red, too?" asked Benny, looking at the claws.

"Sure," said Captain Daniel. He opened the lobster pot and took out three lobsters. He threw one back into the ocean. "Too small," said Captain Daniel. "We'll let it grow some more." The other two he put into the box.

"Don't pick them up, Benny," warned Henry. "You've got to look out for those big claws."

Captain Daniel baited the lobster pot with old fish-heads, shut it, and let it down again into the water. Then he started the motor, and away they went.

"The one who sees the next float first gets all the lobsters in it," said Captain Daniel.

"What color is it?" asked Benny.

"Oh, that would be telling. Each one is a different color," answered the captain.

All the children stared hard at the water. They could see nothing but waves.

"Ho, isn't that another float?" said Henry suddenly, as they went past a blue board.

"Yes, that's one," said the captain. "I hope there will be lobsters in it."

Henry caught the blue float. "Pull hard," said the captain. "It's deep here and there will be more rope. Want any help?"

"No," said Henry. It was hard work. The rope seemed to go straight to the bottom of the ocean. At last the lobster pot came in sight.

"Empty!" cried Jessie. "Too bad!"

"Yes," said Captain Daniel, taking in the lobster pot. "It often happens. This is the best one some days. Do you notice that the bait is gone?"

He baited the pot again and let it down.

"The next one will be yours, also, Henry. Hope for better luck," said the captain.

Soon Benny said, "This float is white. Or maybe it's a wave."

"No, it's a float," said Captain Daniel, laughing. "Henry will have to give you a lobster for finding this float."

Everyone watched as Henry pulled in the lobster pot. At last it came to the top.

"Oh, there are a lot!" cried Henry. "It's a pile of claws. There must be four lobsters. No, five!"

"Six!" said Jessie, as Captain Daniel dropped them one by one into the box. "Isn't that enough for our dinner? Six lobsters? You and Joe will have to come to dinner, too, to help us eat them."

"Yes, thank you, and I'll boil them for you," said Captain Daniel. "I have a big wide kettle. When you take the meat out of the shells it is ready to eat."

"But I don't know how to take the meat out," said Jessie.

"Joe will show you," said the captain.

"Let's do it outdoors," said Jessie.

After they had pulled in a few more lobster pots, Captain Daniel headed the boat back to the island.

"You caught fifteen lobsters," said Benny. "That's a lot!"

"Not very many," said the captain when they had reached the island again. "Some days I get two or three dozen. And six of these lobsters are yours."

When the lobsters had been cooked, Joe sat down on the sand with his young cousins to take out the lobster meat. Jessie and Henry worked, but Violet and Benny just watched.

While they were working, Benny said, "Please let me come when they blow the top off the cave."

Joe looked a little worried. He remembered what had happened before when he said "No." And so he said, "Benny, I'm sorry, but only the ones who will do the work can come."

"Will you be here?" asked Violet.

"Yes, Violet. I have to come. You see this is my work. All the things will go in a museum bigger than

Uncle James' museum. You found some wonderful things."

"Oh, Joe, I'd like to have this for my work, too!" said Henry. "Would you teach me?"

"Yes, Henry, I'd like to. You never can tell what will happen. We might work together."

"Will you tell us everything the men find?" asked Jessie.

"Oh, my, yes!" replied Joe. "You can see every single thing after they have dug it out. I'm glad you don't feel too bad about not doing the digging."

"We understand," said Henry. "It will be better this way."

"Now the lobster meat is all out," said Jessie. "How shall we fix it, Joe?"

"Some people like it cold," began Joe.

"Oh, but I want to cook just once more on the stove," cried Jessie.

Joe smiled. "Then have a stew. Put the lobster meat in milk with butter and salt, and eat it hot."

"That sounds good," said Jessie.

The stew was delicious. When they were eating, Henry said, "I have an idea. Let's come back here weekends until it gets too cold to come."

"Wonderful," said Jessie. "Now we won't have much packing to do. We've eaten all the food."

Violet put the dishes in the cupboard while Jessie put the towels and blankets in boxes to be taken home and washed. Henry stood the rest of the boxes along the wall and shut all the windows. They left the museum just as it was.

Benny carried Violet's paints, pen, and her work-bag. She carried the violin herself.

"Good-by, barn!" said Benny, when Henry shut the door. "I am not going to cry."

"Good for you, Benny!" said Henry. "Just keep thinking how lonesome Grandfather has been."

"I want to go home now," said Benny. "I want to sleep in my real bed."

Henry laughed. A real bed seemed very good to him, too.

Captain Daniel took the children over to the

mainland. When they saw their grandfather waiting for them in the car, they ran to him and all began to talk at once.

"Get in, get in!" said Mr. Alden. "I want to hear all about it, but I can't understand four people all talking at the same time."

But the children could hardly wait to take turns. They told him about the floats and the lobsters and the cave.

"They are going to blow the top off the cave, Grandfather!" cried Benny.

"Really?" said Mr. Alden, who of course knew all about it. "What a noise that will make!"

"Joe won't be home for good until later," said Jessie. "He said to tell you that he would stay with Captain Daniel. He won't move into the little yellow house."

"I should say he won't!" cried Mr. Alden.

For a minute, the children were too surprised to say anything.

Then Henry said, "Grandfather, that's one thing we can't understand. Why didn't we ever get to go into that little yellow house? Doesn't it belong to you?"

Mr. Alden looked at his grandchildren. Then he said quietly, "That's another story."

"We won't ask about it now," said Jessie quickly. "You have been so wonderful to us. Thank you for our summer on the island."

"That's all right," said Mr. Alden, smiling again. "I'm glad to have you all at home. I believe I shall even be glad to hear Watch bark at the milkman tomorrow morning."

That night, when Jessie was going to bed in her own room, she thought she heard Benny calling.

"Did you call me, Benny?" she asked, going into her little brother's room.

"Yes," said Benny very slowly, for he was almost asleep. "I said Joe is going to live with us, and he's my best friend in all the world."

"Yes, I know he is," said Jessie, pulling up the blanket.

"I mean all but you, Jessie, of course, and Violet, and Grandfather—"

"And Watch?" asked Jessie.

"Yes, of course Watch, and Henry—"

He stopped.

"And Captain Daniel—"

Jessie saw that Benny's eyes were shut. He had gone to sleep naming his friends. But it did not matter, thought Jessie, smiling. For it would have taken a long time to name all of Benny's friends.

And downstairs, the children's real best friend settled back in his big chair to make plans for them.

GERTRUDE CHANDLER WARNER discovered when she was teaching that many readers who like an exciting story could find no books that were both easy and fun to read. She decided to try to meet this need, and her first book, *The Boxcar Children*, quickly proved she had succeeded.

Miss Warner drew on her own experiences to write the mystery. As a child she spent hours watching trains go by on the tracks opposite her family home. She often dreamed about what it would be like to set up housekeeping in a caboose or freight car—the situation the Alden children find themselves in.

When Miss Warner received requests for more adventures involving Henry, Jessie, Violet, and Benny Alden, she began additional stories. In each, she chose a special setting and introduced unusual or eccentric characters who liked the unpredictable.

While the mystery element is central to each of Miss Warner's books, she never thought of them as strictly juvenile mysteries. She liked to stress the Aldens' independence and resourcefulness and their solid New England devotion to using up and making do. The Aldens go about most of their adventures with as little adult supervision as possible—something else that delights young readers.

Miss Warner lived in Putnam, Connecticut, until her death in 1979. During her lifetime, she received hundreds of letters from girls and boys telling her how much they liked her books. And so she continued the Aldens' adventures, writing a total of nineteen books in the Boxcar Children series.

